SHATTERED DREAMS

BY

COREY JACKSON

Shattered Dreams. Copyright © 2022 by Corey Jackson.

All rights reserved. Printed in the United States of America. No part of this book may be used or reproduced in any manner whatsoever without written permission, except in the case of brief quotations in critical articles and reviews.

Published by Dream Builders University Press.
Cover design by Gabe Collins.

ISBN: 978-1-947490-13-0

DEDICATION

To James Posey, we laughed together, and we cried together. When you were murdered on September 29, 1989, part of me died with you. The part that didn't die represents you every day. It's tattooed in my heart or tattooed on my arm. I Love You My Nigga.

R. I. P.

SPECIAL ACKNOWLEDGMENTS

I want to thank Aleatha Shaw for making my time behind the fence a very exciting experience and being that silver lining in the midst of all the sadness from missing our freedom. I'm forever grateful to you. Michelle Peterson who through it all never turned her back on me and rode miles after miles to assure I had a relationship with my children my true first ride or die. Romeo Cross and GM Khalid Ashanti Raheem 1 my brothers whom will ride or die for me and have shown it over and over again. Without y'all I don't know where I would be, love y'all. Sean Sincere Finnell and Mike Dog Sanders, every day in that concrete jungle we made it happen, we took that fence to another level and developed a bond that would never be broken. Patrick Moody and Carl Chew Brown thanks for giving my fictional characters names and being a part of this process, much love. And last but not least my wife Trina Jackson, because of you pushing and pushing me to get this book published my book is now a reality, love you boo. And there are many more who played a part in this book and my life, to all my family and friends I love y'all and thanks for the support, love and inspiration.

PROLOGUE

Marie Jenkins was an intelligent, naive, 14-year-old with a dark, creamy-chocolate complexion. She wore black framed glasses, which made her kind of look like a nerd. And in some ways, you could say she was; her only focus in life was school, and making a better life for herself. She always did the right thing and never made bad decisions. However, she was only human and like any human prime to making bad choices, she made a bad choice. One that would change her life forever.

Marie lived in a big brick house on a street called Hale Ave. with her mother Fran, who was a beautiful woman in her own right. She was hard working and made sure her children had everything they needed. Fran was what the world called a "strong black woman". She was strict but also fair and very understanding. Which for Marie, was a good thing because soon she would need that understanding and guidance.

Marie also had two brothers and two older sisters who had a huge influence on her life.

Brenda was ten years older than Marie and protected Marie from the inevitable harassment that most of the young people who put education first received. Brenda was strong willed and not to be fucked with, and even though she was a woman of small stature, she was dangerous. She carried a knife in her bra and a gun in her purse and would use them in the blink of an eye. Her only regret in life was that she was not able to have children. This sometimes hurt her, and often she wished that she'd never went to that party. The party where she was attacked by six girls because none of them could beat her one on one. She often wished God would give her another chance, but she knew that was not possible. And this made her bitter. People would say that she hated everything and everybody, but through Marie's choices, she would find one thing she would love more than herself.

Shelly was only a few years older than Marie. She always had to be the center of attention. She constantly nagged at

Marie to get out of the house and do things, but Marie was a loner and didn't like being around a lot of people. Every time Shelly tried to get Marie out of the house, she would always make up some excuse about some homework or project she must complete. Shelly knew she was making excuses but did not want to push her too hard because Marie was sensitive and could easily be pushed to boys and into doing things all girls do, even the nerds, when pressured. What she did not know was that sooner would come before later, and her nagging would be the reason why Marie's life would change forever.

Mark was the baby of the family. He was laid back, cool and calm, never getting into any trouble. He had one true friend in the world, Jay was his name, and he was the only man in the world with enough game to bring Marie out of her shell.

Lastly was Stoney Jenkins, he was America's worst nightmare: handsome, confident, arrogant and dangerous. He was what every mother feared their children would become. Often, Fran would sit and pray for her son. Marie would sometimes sit with her and hope that if she ever had a son, he would not grow up to be like her brother. She loved her brother dearly, but deep inside she knew that he was evil.

Marie never understood how the streets could make someone so mean. She used to hear about all the things her brother did and could not believe it, because at home, he was so sweet and caring.

One day the phone rang, and Fran fell to the ground in tears. Marie standing at the kitchen sink saw this and ran to her mother's side. The brother whom she had hoped her son would not grow up to be like, was dead. Stoney was stabbed to death at a bar. Those words would haunt her forever, because when life is destroyed, another is created and often in the image of the one closest to the one who was hurt by the loss.

It was Friday night, Male High School was playing a game against Central High School, which was the biggest rivalry in High School basketball in the state of Kentucky and probably the world. Shelly had to cheer and wanted to get her baby sister out of the house because she never went anywhere.

"Marie," she said, "Why don't you come to the game with me tonight?"

"I don't know, I got a lot of homework to do," Marie replied trying to make an excuse.

"For God's sake it's Friday! You got all weekend to do your homework. Stop being such a nerd all the time," Shelly said, shaking her head and rolling her eyes in frustration at her sister.

Marie, not wanting her sister to be angry with her, decided it would be easier to just go to the stupid game. "Okay!"

That night at Male High School, the gym was sold out. You could barely stand anywhere without touching somebody. Marie was feeling extremely uncomfortable and by the end of the first quarter, she was ready to leave. Unfortunately, Shelly who was her only ride home, was still cheering.

By halftime, with Central leading at 42-26 points, tempers were starting to flare, and what everyone knew was going to happen, was already in the air. At the start of the fourth quarter with the game well out of reach now, it was getting ugly. There had already been four or five fights between the girls and boys representing their schools.

Marie was nervous. She had never seen anything like this in her life and she was scared to death. By the end of the game, all hell had broken loose and it was fights everywhere. Marie frantically looked for Shelly but could not find her, and with all these going on around her, she did not know what to do and began to panic. She was almost hit by several flying punches. So, when she felt someone grab her arm, she was ready to fight, even though she has never had a fight in her life. She heard the person behind the arm call her name and when she turned around, she was relieved at the face that she saw. It was Jay. Her brother's best friend.

Jay was the star of Central High School's basketball team and one of the best basketball players in the state of Kentucky. Everybody knew him. Every girl wanted him. He knew this and took full advantage of it. He was 6'3" with short wavy hair and eyes that could make any female drop their panties without knowing they were taking them off.

Many times, Jay would playfully tell Mark; "I want your sister Marie."

"My sister doesn't want you. She knows that you're a dog!" Mark would reply hotly, to which they would both laugh and throw playful punches at each other.

Friday morning, Jay saw Mark in the hall and stopped him asking, "You coming to the game tonight? You know it's going to be off the hook. Everybody is going to be there."

"You know I'm not with that crowd shit. Plus, Male's going to kick y'all asses anyway." Mark said. That was odd, because where Mark did not like crowds, Jay loved them and yet they were best friends. Guess opposites do attract.

"Not if I can help it." Stated Jay as a matter of fact. "If I don't put up 40 points tonight, Popeye is a sissy and so are you." he laughed and ran down the hall. "Plus, tell Marie to come to the game so I can show off."

"Fuck you!" Mark said jokingly. "How many times I got to tell you my sister ain't looking at You?!" He shouted as Jay disappeared around the corner.

Jay sat in the locker room listening to music, getting himself ready for the game. Although he knew he was good, games like this always put a lot of pressure on him.

By halftime, Jay already had 26 of Central's 42 points and tied Male's 26 points by himself. Everything he threw up went in. It was like something was inspiring him and he didn't know what it was. In the middle of the fourth quarter, he was at the free throw line facing the visitor's side of the gym shooting for his 44th point, when he looked up into the crowd and saw Marie looking at all the things going on around her. He could see the fear in her eyes, and knowing that she was not used to this chaotic atmosphere, he felt sorry for her. Out of all the women at his disposal, Marie was the one that he really wanted.

When the final horn sounded, all hell broke loose. Jay didn't even grab his warmup uniform, he ran straight to where he saw Marie sitting. For some reason, he felt like he had to protect her. He raced through the crowd, dodging punches until he reached her. He reached out and grabbed her arm. She turned, ready to punch him until he called out her name, "Marie, it's me Jay, Mark's friend. Come on, let us get out of here before they kill us both!"

He led her outside and went on to take her home. She had never been so happy in her life to see her house. Shelly was not there yet, and this worried Marie. She waited up for her and then finally, she came home and hugged her sister. "Marie, I am so sorry, I shouldn't have ever talked you into coming to that game." Shelly said with tear filled eyes.

"That's okay Shelly," Marie said hugging her sister back. Just happy that she was okay. "I'm home and safe." They both smiled at each other.

"How'd you get home anyway?" Shelly asked suspiciously.

"Mark's friend Jay," Marie replied.

"He likes you, you know that, right?" Shelly told her sister with a grin

"Nah, he was just helping me because of Mark," Marie replied with a dismissive wave.

"If you say so. Come on girl, let's go to bed," Shelly said putting her arm around Marie. "You've got a lot to learn."

For the next year, Jay and Marie were always together. All the other girls hated Marie because she had what they wanted: Jay, and more so because he was no longer interested in anybody else.

Time went by quickly and Marie noticed her period was late. She became scared because of this. She knew she had been taking her birth control pills faithfully, but she understood the pill wasn't 100 percent. She made an appointment with the doctor and her worst fears were confirmed. She was pregnant.

Marie was sitting on the porch when Jay pulled up. He walked up to her and gave her a kiss.

She wasn't herself and Jay could sense it, because she always glowed when he was around. "What's wrong, baby?" Jay asked with concern, feeling like maybe he'd done something wrong.

"Nothing," Marie replied, trying to fight back tears and trying hard not to show her fear that Jay would be angry she was pregnant.

"Marie, don't tell me nothing. I've been around you long enough to know when something is wrong. I know when you're happy and when you're sad and right now, you're sad. So, what is it baby?"

Looking in Jays eyes she knew that he loved her, and he has proven it repeatedly. Never once had she heard or seen him cheating on her or disrespecting her with another female. He'd always been patient and understanding, even when it came to sex. He never pressured her and waited until she was ready. "Jay, I'm pregnant," she finally said.

"Pregnant!" Jay said in total surprise. "How? I mean I know how, but I thought you were on the pill."

"I am, well I was, but you know that's not 100 percent." she said waiting for Jay to respond.

Jay never once thought that Marie was trying to trap him. Someone else maybe, but not Marie and he knew that he was the only one that she has ever been with. "Have you told your mother?"

"Yeah, she knows," answered Marie, expecting a more different response. Shelly had schooled her on how guys are. Though she knew Jay knew he was the only one she's been with, she assumed he would try to deny it.

"What did she say?"

"She was upset. But you know my mother, she understands stuff happens. But if I were you, I'd stay away for a while," Marie said with a small smile knowing that Jay was going to take those words seriously.

On hearing this, Jay immediately turned to look at the door. Making sure Mrs. Jenkins wasn't in the door, Jay turned to Marie; "Good thinking, 'cause I know right now she wants to kick my ass. She doesn't have anything to worry about though, cause I'm going to take good care of you and our child. When I go Pro, you and the baby ain't going to want for shit."

He looked around one more time, then kissed Marie and left to go to practice. Before he pulled off, he let the window down, "I love you Marie and I'll always be there for you and our child." Marie would later learn that promises could be broken. However, it only makes you stronger.

The night before Thanksgiving they rushed Marie to the hospital. Her water broke.

Thanksgiving morning, she gave birth to a 7-pound 9-ounce baby boy. As her and Jay looked down at the baby boy she held tenderly in her arms, Jay asked, "what are we going to name him?"

"I don't know, what should we name him?" she responded, not taking her eyes off her son.

"I don't want to name him after me because I want him to grow up and put his own name on this city like I'm doing. I got a feeling he's going to be something special, probably a football player. Look at him, he's already got muscles," Jay said smiling down at his baby boy.

"How about Cordell?" she said, and Jay shook his head in approval.

"Cordell Jenkins!" repeated Jay, "That sounds like a star."

Marie took Cordell home from the hospital three days after he was born, which was on her 16th birthday. "This is the best birthday present I ever got," she said crying with happiness.

How could she have known that this beautiful baby boy would grow up and give her so much joy with his accomplishments. Then cause her so much heartache with his ruthless and vengeful attack on the streets of Louisville, Kentucky.

She could never stop loving him, even when he made it hard for her to. He reminded her so much of her brother, Stoney, who was killed, but here he was, reincarnated in Cordell Lamont Jenkins, and the world wouldn't be ready for it.

CHAPTER 1

Cordell was sitting in his cell at a federal prison located in Lexington, Kentucky waiting on his visit. He looked around the medium sized cell and took in all the details like it was his first time there. The room had a steel sink and a connected toilet, a steel door with a tray slot; just in case they had to lock down the prison for any number of reasons, the guards could still feed the inmates without having to have direct contact with them. This was good, especially in a cause where a riot would jump off and the guards' life would be in danger. However, in the Federal system, that doesn't happen too often. Most of the big fights are between the Mexican Mafia from California and Texas.

The walls of the room were off white, and the floor was painted gray. The only way to see yourself was through a steel plate used as a mirror that hung on the wall. "Whoever said that Federal prison is better than the State ones must not have been to the Feds." Cordell said to himself as he thought about the luxury of doing State time over Fed time. In the State you could have your own T.V., C.D. player and even PlayStation 2! In the Feds, you had to go to the T.V. rooms; one for sports, one for movies and one for general use. Your only music was a radio. "The food is better though, and the other inmates in the Feds are better. Other than that, I'd rather do State time any day, than do Fed time," Thought Cordell.

He looked at his watch as he was starting to get worried. It was ten minutes till nine and Gina was yet to arrive. For any other inmate this probably wouldn't have been a concern, but for him it was because she was never late. She was always the first one or close to it through the gate and the last one to leave it.

As he thought about his Gina or lil mama, as he liked to call her, a smile came to his face. For five years she had been his rock in the midst of this storm. She never missed a visit or phone call. If she wasn't home, her phone call was always transferred to her cell phone. She would bring his daughter to see him every other weekend and was a wonderful stepmother to her, even though they weren't married. "That would all change once I get out," he promised himself, and one thing he never did was break a promise. To him his word, his honor and his loyalty are the most important things in life.

He got off his bed and walked to the office where Smiley was sitting reading the paper. Smiley was one of the few officers that got along with the inmates. He never put you down and always showed you respect. On some occasions, he would even argue with other officers if he knew that the inmate was right.

"Hey Smiley," Cordell said entering the office, "have they called me for a visit yet?"

"No not that I know Mr. Jenkins." Smiley called everyone Mr. or Sir and made you feel like a human being instead of an animal like some of the other officers did.

"Could you do me a favor and call the visiting room to see if she's here?" asked Cordell.

"I'm sure if she was here, they would have called you, but I'll call to make sure. You know how they are down there sometimes," Smiley said then picked up the phone and dialed, he asked if Cordell's visitor was around yet, listened, then.put the phone back down on the receiver. "No, Mr. Jenkins, she's not here yet. I'll let you know as soon as they call me."

Gina was stuck in traffic and knew Cordell was worried about her. "I know that he is losing his mind right now. I'm surprised my cellphone isn't ringing off the hook," she said to herself.

There was an accident and one whole lane was closed. She looked at her watch; it was 8:20. She usually gets there about 8:00 and is the first through the door at 8:30. She thought about all the trips that she had made on this highway. She could get to the prison and back home blind folded. Through all those trips, this would be the first time she has ever been late, she thought. As if the car in front of this long line could hear her, she yelled "come on, move it damn it, I'm trying to see my baby." She kept looking at her watch and time seemed to be moving extremely fast. "It's always like that when you don't want it to," she muttered. Finally, traffic picked up a little only to slow down again. "This can't be happening, I got to be dreaming."

It had been five years she'd been making these trips faithfully. Every weekend and every holiday. Lucky for her, she won't have to make these trips for ten more years because he gets out in four months. The traffic started moving and she finally got on her way.

At 9:05, she pulled into the parking lot of the prison. She got her mirror out of her purse and checked what little make up she did have on. She didn't have to wear it because her skin was flawless, but she still wore eyeliner and lipstick. Occasionally, she'd put some other stuff on. She checked her hair, which she had gotten done yesterday. It was in these swirly curls that she didn't particularly like, but Cordell loved them, and she would do anything to please her man.

Satisfied with the way she looked, she got out of the car and walked up to the guard station. The officer didn't have to ask her who she was here to see because he already knew. She had been up there so much she was on first name basis with many of the officers. She was escorted into the visiting room by another officer she knew by name, where she waited for Cordell to come out.

"Jenkins, you got a visit," yelled Smiley. Cordell looked at his watch, it was 9:30, "Damn, about time!" he said as he looked himself over one more time, then went to the office to get his pass.

On the way to the visiting room, Paul stopped him. Paul was one of the many inmates who played the parlay ticket Cordell put out every weekend. "How many points was New England giving Miami?" Paul asked.

"If I'm not mistaken, 17. But they should be giving them sorry motherfuckers, 30," Cordell said.

"You say that every week," Paul told him.

"Holler at my runner and make sure that spread is right," Cordell said while still walking to the visiting room.

When he pushed the button on the wall outside the door, he heard a click. He pulled the door open and stepped inside. Once inside he had to be patted down by an officer to make sure he didn't bring anything with him from off the yard that he wanted to get out to the free world. That was stupid. He never understood why they did that, 'cause everything he wanted was out there and wished like hell he could get it in here.

After that was over and the officer was satisfied he didn't have anything he was trying to sneak out, he was led through another door. He looked across the room and saw his lil mama, all the anger he felt about her being late was gone. He walked over and gave her a hug and a kiss.

"I was worried about you," he stated as he gazed into her beautiful eyes.

"I know, I'm sorry!" she said. "It was that damn traffic. All the times I've been up here, the highway ain't never been crowded and today some fool wants to total a new beamer."

"Knew it had to be something cause my baby always on time. I was starting to think Jodi got a hold of you last night," Cordell said, smiling. Jodi was a name inmates gave the other dude who was wining and dining with their girls while they were locked down. Whether his name was Ronnie, Bobby, Ricky or Mike, to the men in prison whose girls these niggas were long-dicking, his name was Jodi.

"Boy quit playing, you know this here pussy belongs to Big Daddy only," Gina said meaning every word of it.

"No that's right and I can't wait to get out and claim what's mine."

"Claim it! Why you got to claim something you never lost?" she said rolling her eyes at him.

"I feel you. But fuck that, go get Big Daddy something to eat, I'm starving."

When Gina got up Cordell could see she had on some black jeans that was so tight you could see her panty line. He didn't know what brand she was wearing, but he knew they were the real deal, 'cause the name was on the inside not the outside. Plus, his baby wouldn't wear nothing but the best. She had on a white shirt that fitted tightly around her large breasts that made his dick get hard instantly. He checked to see if the guard was watching. He noticed he wasn't, so he slapped her on her ass as she walked pass.

"You better quit before you get in trouble," she said and brushed off her ass teasing him. He smiled and watched her walk away.

"Damn! I can't wait until I get home. I miss the hell out of watching her walking around in her bra and panties," He said to himself.

There wasn't a large selection of things Cordell liked out of the vending machine, but his girl knew his taste and got a swiss chicken sandwich, bag of grippos and a big red. Gina warmed up the sandwich as she looked at her man. "Damn, four more months and this shit will be over," she thought.

She grabbed the sandwich out of the microwave and brought the food and put it in front of Cordell. "If you want something else just let me know."

"This will be cool for now," he said as he opened the chips and pulled the tab on the pop. "So, did you check on that information I asked you to get?"

"Yeah, I got it, and everything is going to be ready when you get out," Gina said.

"You talk to Moody and Chew?" he asked. Moody and Chew were two guys Cordell met during his first bit in prison. Together they formed a crew called B.B.C. Black Billionaires Club.

"Moody was kind of uneasy about it and said it would draw too much heat, but Chew was all for it like always," answered Gina.

"I figured that much. Moody is always thinking with logic, where Chew is always about putting in work," he said, taking a sip of his pop.

"Cordell, are you sure you want to do this as soon as you come home?"

"Hell yeah! I've been waiting five years to get that nigga even if it's the last thing I do on this earth! That nigga's going to pay for getting on the stand on me." His eyes were blood shot as he said the words. She knew once his mind was made up there is no changing it, so she just started talking about other things for the rest of the visit.

The officer at the desk told everyone time was up. Cordell grabbed Gina and kissed her passionately, like it was the last time he was going to see her. When he let her go, she looked at him with a question and a soft smile in her eyes; "Boy, why you always kiss me at the end of these visits like you're never going to see me again?"

"Shit baby, in this mad house you never know, niggas be tripping and if a nigga is slipping, it could be his last day."

"Go on with that shit. You know them fools know who you are and they ain't trying to go that route with you."

"Yeah I know, lil mama, but a lot of these cats ain't from Louisville and don't know who they fucking with. Feel me?"

"Boy, I love you!" She said as she turned to walk towards the door.

"I love you too lil mama," he said as he watched her leave.

This was always the hardest part of the visit. Often, Cordell would find himself rubbing his eyes. But the best thing about it was that it was almost over.

He got in line because they had to be searched again. "Now this I can understand. 'Cause if I wasn't so short to the world, I'll be bringing all kinds of contraband back," he thought, thinking about all the money he made at the beginning of his time, when he was bringing shit in off visits like this. When he got back to his cell, his buddy, some white dude out of Frankfort, Kentucky, was walking down the hallway.

He was a Tennessee Titan fan. They were doing good this year. He stopped at Cordell's door. "Titans 10-0 baby. We're going to the Superbowl!" he yelled.

"Damn them bum motherfuckers won again. They got to be paying the refs off," Cordell implied.

"Naw baby, this our year, we going to the Superbowl. How was your visit and that fine caramel candy of yours? If I were into black girls, I would take her from you," he said jokingly.

Hog was a country boy who had never been around blacks, until he did some time down south. Though he was a white boy in the middle of an African jungle, he held his own. He put a lot of money in Cordell's pocket, trying to bust his head on the tickets. He couldn't bet his way out of a wet paper bag, but he was still Cordell's dog.

"Visits are always good when I can hold and touch my woman. As far as you taking her away from me, your dick ain't big enough," said Cordell.

"Don't believe the rumors about white boys and small dicks because they don't call me hog head for nothing, and it ain't this big motherfucker on my shoulders," Hog said, and they both started laughing.

"You stupid man," Cordell said as Hog walked away from his door. "Hey Hog, what was New England's score?"

"Who were they playing?"

"Miami."

"Shit, they got their asses handed to them. I think Miami won like 45-21."

"That's good, now I can rest cause the other tickets ain't got but a few dollars on them," Cordell said.

"If you need any more scores, holla at me, I'll be in the sports TV room," said Hog. "Plus, you ain't going to keep getting away. Next week I'm going to bust your head, if you ain't careful with them spreads."

"Yeah right, you couldn't bust yourself out of a wet paper bag. Shut my door."

"I'll holla!" Hog said and walked off.

Cordell turned his radio on and laid on his bed. He thought about what Gina had told him. If everything went the way he had planned in four months, he would get his revenge as he promised he one day would. He couldn't believe that ratting ass nigga he thought was his friend and trusted so much, tried to put him in prison for the rest of his life. "I shared everything with that nigga, and this is how he repays me. I should've killed him a long time ago. Chew tried to warn me, but I didn't want to listen. Now look at me," he said to himself with hate in his heart.

    He put his hands behind his head looking at the ceiling. He started thinking back to where it all began. When he first allowed his pride, ego and emotions to shatter his dreams which eventually got him to this present moment in his life. He closed his eyes, and as the room began to get dark, he went back 14 years.

CHAPTER 2
14 YEARS AGO

It was Monday. As the players were heading out of the locker room to the practice field to prepare for their season opener, Cordell, still upset by the events that took place Friday night in a scrimmage game against Doss High School, sat still. A lot of his friends played for Doss, including some of his arch-rivals from when he played in the youth football league from his younger days.

Though some of them had grown bigger than him, it was his chance to show them that he was still the best and he still owned them, because the football field was his home. He knew he would never get another chance because the schools didn't play each other in the regular season as they were in different districts. For him, this was his last chance because he was a senior.

Leo, his best friend since their freshman year - which is ironic because at one time they'd been sworn enemies - played for the opposing team. The teams they each played for hated each other. It was mostly between the coaches, but it spilled onto the players. However, somehow, he and Leo were able to put that behind them and for the past three years, became a combo to be reckoned with. In fact, sometimes on the field during games, it was hard to tell them apart. Even the announcer used to get them mixed up. Cordell wore number 3 and Leo wore number 33. They both had killer instincts that made them excel in this man-on-man brutal sport.

"What's up Cordell?" Leo said as he was heading out of the locker room. "You alright? It looks like you're ready to kill somebody. Please remember this is practice. Try not to hurt nobody 'cause we open the season on Friday."

"I'm alright, I just don't understand that bitch ass coach we got. How the fuck can he hold me out of that scrimmage?" asked Cordell.

"Man, he was only doing what's best for the team. You know we can't afford for you to get hurt before the season starts. Shit, you're our only hope for the championships."

"Fuck that!" Cordell shouted. "If I don't take hits now what's going to happen when them big, cornbread eating motherfuckers from St. X hit my ass on Friday. I haven't been touched all summer!"

"I feel you, but hopefully them big motherfuckers ain't hitting you. That means you're scoring touchdowns, and we're winning," Leo said as he walked out of the locker room.

Cordell was the last one out of the locker room and to the field. Coach Kendricks saw something was wrong with his star player, especially since he's always jumping in everybody else's ass for being late.

Coach Kendricks walked over to Coach Bush with his eyes still on Cordell. "What's up with Cordell? He seems a little unfocused."

"I don't know, he was like that Friday during the scrimmage, kinda stayed to himself," Coach Bush said staring at Cordell.

"That ain't like him. He's usually busting his ass and jumping on everybody else, especially with Friday being the season opener against the number one team in the state."

"Maybe the pressure is hitting him." Coach Bush stated.

"No, I doubt that I've ever seen that boy allow pressure to faze him. If anything, it motivates him," Kendricks said, knowing that a game like this brings the best out of Cordell because he hates to be second.

Coach Kendricks thought back to the first time he saw Cordell. He was a small black kid, compared to the other black kids he had on his team. It was three years ago, during a JV and Varsity practice. He walked on the field like he was the biggest football player you ever saw and said that he wanted to play. Coach looked at the small kid and admired his heart.

"I think you're looking for the freshman practice, that ain't till 6:30," he told Cordell.

"I don't mean no disrespect Coach, but I don't want to play with no kids. I want to play varsity," Cordell stated with confidence.

He laughed at Cordell. "Kid, I admire your heart, but around here everybody starts over on the freshman team, their freshman year."

It was obvious that he didn't know what he'd done. He started a fire inside of Cordell. Because one thing he hated was somebody to not believe in him. He promised himself that he was going to make Coach Kendricks eat those words and that was on his word, which he never breaks.

As he looked at Cordell and saw how the years had changed his body since that first game the freshman team played, where Cordell punished everything he touched as the Varsity coaches and players looked on, he had no choice but to break his rules and move Cordell up to the Varsity team as his starting outside linebacker. There was no doubt in his mind that Cordell would someday be a millionaire because the skills he possessed were beyond anything he had ever seen. One day he would be a star in the NFL and he could say that he had coached him.

Since that day, his team went from pretenders to contenders and now he had a chance to coach a State Championship team because Cordell could take them there this year. He'll never ever coach another player like Cordell. This he was sure of. He always stated to himself that "when God made him, he broke the mold." But something was wrong with his star player and he had to break him out of it before Friday night.

A whistle blew bringing Coach Kendricks out of his thoughts. "First team offense take the field," He barked out. As everyone on the first team offense moved to take their places in the huddle, Cordell looked at Tony and said, "Get in there!" Tony looked at him strangely and didn't move. He knew that he was second string and Cordell's back up. Coach Kendricks looked at Cordell, "What are you doing? Get in the huddle!" Cordell shot him an evil look, and said, "I thought you wanted the first team in there?"

Confused, Coach Kendricks said, "What are you talking about? You are on the first team."

"I wasn't Friday night. Plus, I might get hurt. Ain't that what you said Coach?" Cordell said, placing emphasis on the word Coach.

"Come here Cordell, let me talk to you," Coach Kendricks said, beckoning for him with his hands.

"Anything you got to say to me, you can say in front of the team," Cordell said instead.

"Son, you got the potential to be one of the best football players to ever come out of the state of Kentucky and you're worrying about a practice game?" Coach stated. "I got colleges calling me every day for film on you and asking what type of person you are. Everything I tell them is nothing but good. And now you question my judgment because I don't want you to get hurt in a meaningless game?!"

"Meaningless game?!" Cordell shouted. "All of my friends played on that team and now I got to hear how they beat us, and I didn't do shit."

"Is that all you care about Cordell, what you want to do? This is a team and you ain't the only one on it. If you can't realize that, then you have a lot to learn," Coach Kendricks said.

"A team! I put this school on the map! Before I got here, this school wasn't shit! How many games did y'all win before I got here, and how many have y'all won since I've been here? I am this team. And you know what? I don't need y'all. Y'all need me! So, let's see what y'all do without me!" Cordell half yelled.

Everyone looked stunned and couldn't believe what they just witnessed. Leo, sensing his chance to win a championship before he left this school slipped away from the group and ran up to Cordell trying to talk some sense into him. "Man, don't do this to us. This is our last year to win a championship and you know we can't do it without you."

Norm pulled up beside Leo and tried to put his two cents in. "Come on Cordell, I wouldn't even be here if it wasn't for you. You can't walk out on us like that," he said.

Cordell, looking at his two friends thought about what Norm said about not being there if it wasn't for him. He thought back to when they first tried out and Norm's fat ass couldn't make it around the field for the mandatory three laps they had to run. Every day he would catch up with him and help him. He was Cordell's friend.

"I understand that, and I love both of y'all, but you heard what Coach said. You don't need me and I'm going to make him eat those words," Cordell said.

That Friday was the first game of the season, so Cordell decided to go to the game. When he walked up to the gate to pay his money, the attendant recognized him immediately and told him that he didn't have to pay. As he walked to the stands, several girls approached him, which for him, was nothing new. Attention. Everybody in the State of Kentucky knew who he was, and the girls loved him for what he represented.

He found a seat and watched the game. Several times he found himself getting mad, especially when Tony would drop a pass he knew he should've caught. Some of which would've enabled him score a touchdown. His team was losing and for the first time, he regretted his decision. But it wouldn't be the last time.

At halftime, he walked to the gate as his team was leaving the field to go back to the locker room. He saw the looks on their faces as they passed him by. He couldn't help but drop his head, 'cause he knew he'd let them down.

Leo was one of the last ones off the field. He looked up at Cordell and said, "I told you we needed you! Look at this shit! Tony dropping passes, and them running all over us, especially on Dale's side." Dale was Cordell's backup. He was an outside linebacker on the defensive side of the ball. He knew if he was in there, none of that would have been happening. Teams hardly ever ran to his side.

"My fault Leo man, but I can't let nobody play me the way Coach did," Cordell said.

"Cordell, you played yourself. You were supposed to ride this train all the way into college and then the NFL. What you think these college coaches going to think about you now that you quit on your team, man?" Cordell lowered his head and walked off knowing that Leo was telling the truth. But if they wanted him back, Coach Kendricks is going to have to beg him and that was on his word.

Monday at school, it seemed that every person in the whole damn building was mad at him.

"Damn, it was just one game. They will be alright. Now everybody's got an attitude with me," he thought to himself. He was sitting in homeroom in the corner by himself looking out of the window, when he heard: "Cordell Jenkins, come to the Administration Office," over the loudspeaker. "I knew Coach was going to change his tune, he knows they need me," he said as he walked down to the office.

When he got there, the athletic director, principal, and his counselor were the only ones there. His pride and ego were shattered. He just thought that Coach Kendricks would be there begging him to come back and he really wanted to come back.

Mrs. Dunn, the principal, told him to have a seat. "I understand that you and Coach Kendricks had a little problem."

"No. I don't have a problem, he does," Cordell said.

"Young man, you can go places. But if you don't get rid of that ego and attitude of yours, you are not going to be anything," Mr. Thomas the Athletic Director said.

"I ain't got to sit here and listen to this bullshit. During football and basketball season y'all all on my nuts and as soon as that shit is over, I'm just another nigga to y'all."

"Young man, watch your language!" Mrs. Harris, his counselor, whom Cordell kinda liked, shouted. Out of all the people in that room, she was the only one who was there for him when he just needed to talk. He felt bad that she had to be there, and that he put her in the category with the rest.

"I'm sorry Mrs. Harris, but you don't understand. I gave this school my all and they treat me like shit."

"Look at how you're acting," said Mr. Thomas.

Cordell didn't say another word, he just got up and walked out, slamming the door as he left. That day would change Cordell's life forever. Just like he slammed the door that day, many doors will be slammed on him and many more will be opened to him.

CHAPTER 3

Cordell walked into his house to find his mother and father waiting for him. He could understand his mother waiting because he knew the school would call her. What he couldn't understand was what his father was doing there or why his mother would call him. Him and his father did not have much of a relationship. He always felt his father abandoned them and really wanted nothing to do with him. As he sat down on the couch, his mother looked at him and he could see the disappointment in her eyes, and this hurt him deeply. Cordell and his mother had a wonderful relationship. Under no circumstance would he ever lie to her. Wrong or right, her love was unconditional. She was a firm believer of taking responsibility when you do something wrong. But if you were in the right, she would stand up for you at all cost.

"Boy, what is wrong with you?" she asked. "Them people called my job today and told me what you done. Have you lost your damn mind?"

"You don't understand, all them people want to do is use me to play sports," said Cordell.

"Why didn't you use them to go to college?" his father said. "You had all kinds of scholarship offers that you've probably thrown away," he added.

"What do you care. All I hear is my son is this, my son is that, but how many games have you come to? What? Two or three since I was 10 years old?" shouted Cordell. "All these white boys' fathers coming up to me after every game, telling me how good I played, but where was my own damn father?!" Cordell yelled with tears in his eyes as he looked at his father with pure hate.

"Cordell!" his mother shouted, "why are you talking to your father like that?"

"My father! He ain't been my father since I was nine years old. What has he done for us? Nothing! I tried my best to be his son, but has he tried to be my father? Hell no! So, don't start trying now," he said the last part with looking at his father with venom. He then got up and walked out of the house.

His mother looked at his father with tears in her eyes. She had never seen her son so hurt, and she could tell his words tore his father's insides apart. "I'm sorry Jay. I don't know what has gotten into that boy," she said.

"He'll be alright. I can understand why he's mad at me and I can't blame him. I haven't been the best father in the world," said Jay.

She looked at the floor and knew deep inside that Jay wished he could change his relationship with his son. He had been out of his life for too long and Cordell would never forgive him for that. "He reminds me of my brother more and more every day," she said as she got up and walked Jay to the door.

Cordell was at the game room down the street from his house, playing Ms. PAC-man, trying to take his mind off everything that happened today.

"What's up Cordell?" a voice said from behind him. He turned around and saw Rome standing there. Rome and his twin brother were the leaders of a local gang in the neighborhood where he lived. For a while Rome and his crew gave Cordell a hard time, but they saw he wasn't soft and they respected that and left him alone. "What's up Rome?" Cordell said, turning around to finish his game.

"They having a block party over on 38th street on Friday, why don't you roll with us? It's going to be plenty of fine girls there," Rome said.

"Hell, why not, I ain't got shit else to do on Friday night. What time y'all rolling out?"

"About 9:00 or 10:00."

"That punk ass nigga Earl ain't still rolling with y'all is he?" Earl was one of the guys in Rome and his brother's crew that Cordell beat up when he first moved in the neighborhood and they still didn't get along.

"Nah, we don't fuck with him much no more. He's been on some bitch shit lately," said Rome.

Friday came. Cordell had on some hard Levi's, white Polo shirt, and some white on white, Dope man Nike's. He had on a chain his auntie Brenda gave him before she went to prison 10 years ago. It was too big for him then, but now it fit exactly right. He thought about his auntie and wished she was home. She was the only person who really understood him. No matter what he done he was never wrong in her eyes and nobody better not say that he was because she was nuts and would fuck somebody up over her nephew.

When he was five years old his mother tried to give him a whooping for something he had done, his auntie Brenda came in and went straight to her breast and pulled out her knife. She told his mother if she touched him, she'd kill her. From that day on he knew that he could get away with murder, 'cause his auntie Brenda had his back, and she was the baddest bitch.

Four years later, while out drinking, his aunt Brenda shot a lady in the ear for meddling in her conversation. She got 25 years. That was the first time in Cordell's life that he experienced the pains of loss, but it surely wouldn't be the last.

"I got to write my auntie," he said as he touched the chain around his neck. "I know she's mad at me. I haven't written her in a month," he said loudly. He looked at himself one more time and left to go meet Rome and his crew.

Rome and his boys were at the game room waiting on Cordell because Rome likes for them to all walk together just in case there is a problem.

"What's up Cordell?" said Que, one of Rome's boys.

"Shit, not much. Ready to go get my party on and meet some of this fine ass women Rome was hollering about," Cordell said.

"Let's roll then, everybody is here," said Rome. They all gave each other a dap, checked themselves again to make sure they were fly and then headed to the party.

When they got to the party it was sold out. Everybody was there and just as Rome had said, there were all kinds of pretty girls there, Cordell thought to himself. There were some other gangs there as well that really didn't like Rome or his twin brother, so Cordell knew it was possible that some shit could break off. "Fuck it, if it happens it happens," he said and went on about his business.

As he was walking around, he saw this girl who was fine as hell. She was light skinned with long sandy brown hair, and a body that made his manhood rise the moment he laid eyes on it. She was standing with some other girls, one of which he already knew. Her name was Tameka. She had tried to holla at him before, but everybody in the hood done already had her and he didn't roll like that. He walked over to the crowd of girls. Tameka was the first one to say something.

"What's up Cordell? I thought you had a game tonight?" she said.

"Nah shorty, I quit. I'm going to see if I can transfer schools and be eligible by basketball season."

"You did what?!" she exclaimed. "Nigga are you crazy? You had it made. You could've gone to any college you wanted to go to for free, now you fucked that up. That's what's wrong with y'all hood niggas. Y'all stupid."

"Girl, who you calling stupid?" he asked, getting angry.

"You!" she shot back.

"Anyway, who's your friend?" he asked with his eyes on the fine red bone standing there listening to him and Tameka acting like a married couple.

"Why don't you ask her yourself?" said Tameka, then went to get something to drink. He could tell she was upset because he asked about her friend, but fuck her. She shouldn't be. "What's your name baby girl?" he asked in a low sexy voice.

"Ty-chelle," said the redbone.

"My name is Cordell."

"I already know who you are. I saw you last year when you played against my school and you tore our butts up," she said.

"What school you go to?"

"Butler."

"Yeah, I remember that game. I had three touchdowns and eleven tackles. That was one of my best games. Now I know why," he said.

"Why?"

"Cause you was in the stands watching me," Cordell said with a smile on his face that could melt the heart of any female.

"You are silly," she said blushing from ear to ear.

"Nah shorty, forreal. I knew I had to show off 'cause one day I knew we would be standing right here at this exact moment," he said really turning on the charm now, because he knew he had her. Truth be told, he never ever had to say a word to Ty-chelle, but hello and he would've had her.

"You are a trip," she said, thinking back to that game last year when she saw him coming off the field at halftime with his helmet off. She was his then and now she stands face to face with the one boy who has been in her dreams for over a year. The rest of the night went well. There was a couple of arguments and almost fights, but nothing major. Cordell and Ty-chelle kicked it for the rest of the night, making sure that they exchanged numbers before leaving the party.

When he got home, he couldn't help but think of her. He picked up the phone and dialed the number she gave him, hoping it was the right one. Without a doubt, he knew it was, cause he could tell she was feeling him just like he was feeling her. She answered on the second ring, and they talked for four hours about everything they could think of. Even when they ran out of things, one of them thought of something to keep the other on the phone.

When they hung up, the sun was coming up. Cordell laid in his bed looking out of the window. For the first time since he walked off the field, he didn't regret leaving the team and now he knew what school he was going to transfer to.

He decided he'd wait until Sunday night to talk to his mother and let her know his plans. He was sure she wouldn't mind, plus it would be easier on her since she wouldn't have to drop him off at the bus stop every morning like she'd been doing. He closed his eyes and dreamed about Ty-chelle and come Tuesday, he'd be able to see her every day. The thought brought a smile to his face.

Monday morning, Cordell walked into the counselor's office. "I'd like to see Mrs. Harris," he said to the secretary. "She's in with another student right now Cordell, but I'm sure she will only be a minute, so you can have a seat over there," said Mrs. Wilson.

Mrs. Wilson was the secretary, but she wasn't one of those old ladies that you see with the gray hair pinned up with a pencil sticking out of the middle of it. She had long silky black hair, a pointed nose, with black girl lips like Angelina Jolie, and her tan looked like it was painted on her body. He wasn't into white women, but she was beautiful, and Cordell found himself staring at her with lust in his eyes. Rumor was that she was a stripper in this club called the Toy Tiger, but nobody knew for sure. "I could see myself throwing dollar bills on the stage," he thought to himself.

The student who was in with Mrs. Harris walked out and Mrs. Wilson told Cordell to go on in. He got up and walked past her, still not taking his eyes off of her. She noticed him staring at her and smiled at him, and he could've sworn she winked at him.

"Shut the door Cordell," said Mrs. Harris. "What can I do for you?"

"I would first like to apologize to you for the way that I acted last week. Trust me, it wasn't towards you. You have been nothing but helpful to me since I've been here, and I have the upmost respect for you," he said.

"Thank you, I appreciate that, but I know that's not the only reason that you're here, so how can I help you?"

She thought that he was there to talk about rejoining the football team, which would be music to her ears. She liked Cordell and knew he could be something special if he would just put his mind to it. His next words shattered her thoughts.

"I would like to transfer to another school," he said.

"You would like to what?" she asked, confused, not expecting that at all. "I mean why? This is your senior year, and we were hoping you would rejoin the team."

"Mrs. Harris, I gave this school all I had, and Coach didn't appreciate that. When he told me they didn't need me, that ate right through me and I can't see myself playing for him."

"I understand that Cordell, I really do, but you're going to let coach Kendricks stand in the way of you going to college?"

"He's not going to stand in my way. I'm still going to Tennessee, even if I have to pay for my first year and wait for a scholarship."

"It's your life Cordell, and I'm not trying to tell you how to live it, but I feel that you're making a big mistake."

"Mrs. Harris, I got to do what's best for me, and right now, I feel the best thing for me is to transfer schools," He said while looking down at the floor because deep in his heart, he knew that he wanted to play football.

"You seem to have made up your mind. So, what school do you want to transfer to? I'll start with the paperwork."

"Butler High School," he said with a smile on his face, as he thought about Ty-chelle.

"That's a good school. One of my friends is the counselor over there. Mrs. Tate is her name. Just know that I will be checking up on you," she said to him looking over the top of her black framed glasses.

"You don't have to worry about it Mrs. Harris. I'm going to do what I'm supposed to do."

"I know you will Cordell, and I wish you all the luck in the world. The paperwork will be done by the end of the day. You take care of yourself."

"I will. Thank you." He walked out of the office, getting one more look at Mrs. Wilson. "Damn! If only I were four or five years older," he thought as he shut the door behind himself.

Leo and Norm were standing by the lunchroom when Cordell came down the hall. He stopped and talked to them for a minute and told them about his plans. They were a little upset because they too thought that he would come to his senses and come back to the team. "Damn man, I hate to see you go," Leo said.

"Shit, I hate to go, but right now I got to look out for me."

"So, you're going to Butler, huh?" asked Norm.

"Yeah," answered Cordell.

"I heard they got some bad bitches," said Leo. "Plus, I heard they off the chain."

"Nigga, is that all you think about?" asked Norm.

"Shit, what else is there to think about?" Leo replied.

"Your dick's going to fall off," Norm said.

"Look, as much as I enjoy seeing you ladies argue, I got to get to class and so do you," said Cordell. "Alright my nigga, holla at me after third period," Leo said.

"I got you," said Cordell as he walked down the hall to his class.

Cordell's first day at Butler was more than he expected. Everybody knew who he was. The girls looked with admiration and the guys looked with jealousy and envy. There were a few people that he knew from sports and just being out in the hood or at parties. He got along with most of them, but it really didn't matter. There was only one reason why he was here: she walked up behind him and put her arms around him. "What's up boo?" Ty-chelle said.

"Oh, it's Boo now cause of all these females around, right? Is that why you got your arms around me?" asked Cordell.

"Hell yeah! I got to let these bitches know you're mine and if they try me, I will fuck them up."

Cordell started laughing. "Oh, so you're gangsta now that I'm on your turf?"

"Nah Boo, it ain't like that. But I'm not going to play about my man," she said looking up at him.

"Your man? Now I'm your man? Why don't you tell me when it happened?" he said playfully.

"You was my man a year ago after the game, you just didn't know it yet," she said and smacked Cordell on his butt and walked off. "You better get to homeroom."

He watched as she walked down the hall, occasionally looking over her shoulder to smile at him. He shook his head.

"They said these Butler girls were wild. What have I got myself into?" he thought as he started to his homeroom.

Ty-chelle was sitting at her desk when Karen, her best friend, sat down at the desk next to her. "I see you're happy," Karen said while looking at her best friend with envy.

"Yeah girl. He told me that he was coming here, but I didn't believe it until I saw him this morning," said Ty-chelle.

"You better watch out, every girl in this school is talking about that nigga. I didn't realize that nigga was that cute until I got up on him this morning."

"Watch it bitch!" Ty-chelle said playing with her friend. "On the real though, these bitches can play with me if they want to, I'll fuck them up."

"I hear you girl, that nigga is worth fighting over and you just might have to do just that," Karen said.

"I'm not worried about that cause he ain't going to do nothing silly. So, these bitches can try all they want. I trust my man."

"I hear you girl. Do he got any good looking friends?" Karen asked.

"Yeah, he hangs with this dude name Rome who I think you would like."

"Shit, hook me up then."

"I'll holla at Cordell after homeroom."

Over the next couple of months, Ty-chelle and Cordell got even closer. If that was even possible. They spent all their free time together when he wasn't with Rome and his crew.

He couldn't play on the basketball team because he wasn't enrolled there on the first day of school, but that didn't really bother him so much, as football was his true love besides Ty-chelle.

He hooked Rome up with Ty-chelle's best friend, Karen, whom he didn't particularly like. She was always flirting, even with him. But Rome liked her, and she was Ty-chelle's friend, so he tolerated her. The four of them did everything together, even kicked some ass later down the road.

CHAPTER 4

The summer came and everybody was glad for that, especially Cordell. He had talked to his mother and she was going to pay for him to go to college. His mother was a nurse and one thing his granny taught her was how to save money for rainy days. Although she knew Cordell would probably get a scholarship, she wanted to be prepared just in case. So many young athletes get injured and end up out on the streets, so she had been putting money aside cause you never know what could happen.

But one thing is for sure; she was going to make sure her son had an education. So, he knew he could still go to any college he wanted to, but he decided on Tennessee. They were recruiting him heavy and that is where he was going to go anyway. He was going to walk onto the football team his first year, but knew they were going to give him a scholarship after that because they still wanted him.

That weekend, Cordell, Ty-chelle, Rome and Karen were in the mall like all the teenagers on the weekends, especially in the summer. The mall was the next best thing to the club if you wanted to meet somebody or just hang out. They were standing by the Footlocker, looking at some shoes, when this guy came up. He looked at Karen and immediately she could tell it was going to be a problem.

"Bitch! What are you doing with these niggas?" he asked.

Cordell didn't recognize this dude, but Tyrone knew him right off. His name was Capone, and he was the leader of a gang called the Crips. Before that, they were called L.A. because the guy came from there.

"Hold up Capone. How are you going to push up on my girl like that and disrespect me like that?" said Rome, with his hand at Capone's chest.

Cordell, looking at the body language of the two, knew how Rome carried it, moved Ty-chelle to the side because he knew there was going to be trouble and wanted her out of harm's way.

"Nigga, your girl!? She was my bitch before she was your girl and always going to be my bitch," Capone said moving Tyrone's hand.

"I ain't nobody's bitch!" Karen finally spoke up.

Putting his hand up to push her back, Rome said, "Hold up. I got this," then hit Capone with a violent right jab to the mouth.

Capone fell to the ground, Rome and Cordell began to stomp him, even the girls got in some kicks. They saw a crowd of people gathering around and they knew it wouldn't be long before the police came, so they bounced.

When they got back to Cordell's house and knew they were safe, they all sat back and laughed about what they had done.

"Y'all crazy!" Ty-chelle said.

"Shit! Us? Y'all jumped in too," said Cordell.

"He shouldn't have called me a bitch," Added Karen and Ty-chelle gave her a high five.

Rome, knowing who Capone was, knew this was just the beginning. He wasn't going to let this slide.

It was at times like this that Rome wished his twin brother wasn't in jail on those gun charges. He knew Cordell had heart, but not like his brother. He also knew Capone was going to come hard. He looked around at all of them and thought they were laughing now, but he knew that they would be crying later if Capone caught him or Cordell slipping.

He knew he could protect himself, but he was worried about Cordell. Capone wasn't no whore, but he knew he would try to go after the weakest link, which now, was Cordell because he wasn't a banger in the street way.

Capone sat at his clubhouse with some of the members of his crew. His lip was swollen and his eye was black, but you could still see murder in them. His right-hand man, Dino looked at him. "Man, what were you doing slipping like that anyway?" he said. "You know that nigga Tyrone ain't no bitch."

"Fuck Rome! One on one I would've smashed his ass," Capone said. Deep in his heart he believed that, but truth be told, he had no chance against Rome heads up. "If his bitch ass partner wouldn't have jumped in, I would've beaten him to death."

"You're tripping Capone, that bitch Karen got your nose wide open still, and she stopped fucking with you two months ago!"

"Nigga, you got me fucked up! No bitch got my nose wide open. I just hate it when bitches from our hood fuck with niggas from other hoods. Especially a bitch I fucked with!"

"So, you're saying, if it had been a nigga from our hood, you wouldn't have fronted on Karen like that?"

"Yeah, as long as it ain't no nigga that I fuck with," said Capone.

"Alright nigga, whatever," Dino said. "Anyway, what we going to do to these niggas?" He already knew the answer to that but asked anyways. He knew Capone wasn't going to let this ride, especially since he got his ass beat in front of Karen.

"What do you mean what are we going to do?" Capone said with an evil look at Dino. "We going to murder these motherfuckers!" Right then and there Dino knew it was going to be a long summer and a lot of blood was going to be shed. He just hoped it wasn't his.

CHAPTER 5

Ty-chelle picked up the phone to call Karen, it rang a couple of times before she finally answered.

"Hello," Karen said.

"What's up girl?" said Ty-chelle.

"Nothing, sitting over here watching the Young and the Restless, tripping off this fool Victor and his power trip. Motherfucker act like he owns the world. It ain't going to be long before Nicky or Jack shoot his ass again."

"Bitch, you and your soap operas. You make it sound like some shit going on in real life," said an exasperated Ty-chelle. They both laughed.

"What you got planned for today?" Karen asked.

"Nothing forreal, I ain't feeling too good. Stomach hurting, feel like a bitch about to come on."

"Your ass might be pregnant. You know you and Cordell been fucking like crazy and ain't using no protection."

"How do you know what we use?"

"You know I know how fucked up you are about that nigga. I wouldn't be surprised if you're trying to get pregnant on purpose."

Ty-chelle couldn't help but smile. She knew her girl and she was right. She had been trying to get pregnant. Cordell was getting ready to leave for college and she had heard how those college girls were and she wanted to lock him down.

"You are a monkey ass bitch," Ty-chelle said, laughing into the phone. "Well girl, I'm going to let you get back to your soap opera, but if you and Rome ain't doing nothing, why don't y'all stop down Cordell's?"

"I'm going to let you spend some Q.T. aka quiet time with your precious Cordell tonight. Maybe he'll put a baby in your ass, if you're not already pregnant," Karen said. "Me and Rome will probably just sit in and watch a movie."

"Okay girl, love ya!" said Ty-chelle.

"Love you too!" Karen said, and they hung up.

• • •

Cordell and Rome were sitting on Cordell's porch drinking a few beers when Cordell looked at Rome. "You know that nigga Capone's going to come back don't you?"

"I ain't worried about that punk ass nigga. He shouldn't have tried to front in front of that bitch."

"I know you ain't worried my nigga, I just want you to watch your back, cause niggas ain't letting ass whoopings ride these days," Cordell stated matter of factly.

"Watch my back?!" Rome lifted up his shirt and showed Cordell the butt of the .357 he carries with him. "This is my American Express Card. I never leave home without it. While you're talking, you need to strap up because he'll probably come after you before me. He knows you ain't no gang banger and would feel like you're an easier target. That's how those weak niggas think."

"Yeah, I feel you. So, I'm going to need one of those. You got me?" asked Cordell.

"You know I do my nigga. Let me call Tre and get him to drop one off over here now." He picked up his cell phone and dialed a number.

Tre pulled up 20 minutes later and handed Rome a jet black .38 special and a box of hollow point bullets. "Here you go my nigga," Rome said handing Cordell the gun and bullets. "Remember, if you use it, throw that motherfucker in the river somewhere."

Cordell took the gun from Rome's hand, pointed it nowhere in particular and pulled the trigger several times. For the first time in a long time, he felt powerful. The look that came across Cordell's face scared Rome because he could see it in his eyes that he could become a cold-blooded killer.

"Put that up before the police ride pass this motherfucker and we all end up in jail," said Rome still looking at Cordell suspiciously.

Cordell went and put the gun up. As he was on his way back out to the porch, he turned around and ran to the restroom, where he threw up for the second time that morning.

"Damn nigga, what's wrong with you?" Rome asked. "Looking at a gun make your ass throw up? Just wait until you use that motherfucker, you're probably gon' shit your pants."

"Nah man, that's the second time I threw up this morning."

"Shit, you probably got that bitch Ty-chelle pregnant." Rome said.

"First of all, don't call her a bitch!" Cordell said. "Nah, she ain't pregnant, might be something I ate."

"My fault. I forgot she got you pussy whipped."

"So, what's up tonight?" Cordell asked changing the subject.

"Karen wants to watch some movies and suck a nigga dick all night. So, I'll probably chill at her crib until about 1 or 2 o'clock."

"Cool, when you get done, stop back by here and I'll have some cold ones waiting."

"Will do," Rome said, giving his man some dap.

Rome was heading down the steps when Cordell got the strangest feeling in his stomach. "Hey Rome!" Rome turned around and looked up the steps, "be careful man."

Rome waved him off. "Man, I'm not worried about that bitch ass nigga. Like I told you, they'll come after you before they will me."

"Just be careful, superman," said Cordell, shaking his head laughing.

"Alright, man," was the last thing Rome said as he got in his car.

Around 8:30pm, Dino came running to the club house yelling, "Capone, you ain't going to believe this, guess who I just saw?"

"Nigga, who? This ain't no price is right or no shit like that right?" said Capone.

"That nigga Rome up Karen's crib right now."

Capone jumped up, grabbed his 9mm from under the chair where he was sitting. "You got to be shitting me. I know that nigga ain't in my hood after all the shit that went down at the mall! This nigga must think I'm a bitch forreal!"

"I'm telling you man, he's up there right now. Plus, he's by himself," Dino said eagerly.

"Come on!" said Capone, headed for the door with Dino and several other members of his crew trailing behind him.

Rome and Karen were sitting on the couch discussing which movie they wanted to watch first when they heard a knock at the door. Boom! Boom!

"Who is it?" she yelled down the step, but nobody answered. There was another hard knock. Boom! Boom!

"Who the fuck is playing at my door?" Karen asked, running down the stairs.

"It's probably Cordell and Ty-chelle playing games," Rome yelled from behind her still sitting on the couch looking over the movies.

 Karen unlocked the door and snatched it open, and what she saw made her eyes bulge out of her head. She tried to push the door shut, but Capone stuck his foot in it to keep it from shutting.

"Where that punk ass nigga Rome at?" Capone said, trying to push his way in the house.

Rome heard his name and recognized the voice. He jumped up from the couch and grabbed his gun from his waist. He knew there was no need in trying to talk because he knew Capone was a trigger-happy nigga and wasn't going to let that shit at the mall slide.

Karen, not strong enough to hold the door, ran up the steps shouting Rome's name. Capone, pushing his way in, followed by his crew, started up the steps behind Karen. As soon as she cleared the last step Rome fired down on them, hitting one of Capone's boys in the shoulder.

Capone, knowing he was a sitting duck standing on the steps while Tyrone stood at the top firing down on them, motioned for his crew to back out the door. They pulled J-

Rock, who had been hit by Rome's bullet, out of the door and out of the way in case he was going to fire again and finish him off. Capone fired a couple of shots up the steps and Rome fired two more times.

"Bitch, call Cordell cause I ain't got but three bullets left in this fucking gun," Rome said looking helpless.

Karen ran to the phone and dialed Cordell's number, but didn't get an answer. She tried it again, still with no luck. Scared shitless, she tried Ty-chelle's cell phone and still didn't get an answer. Tears started running down her face as she tried both numbers again and again. She heard more gun shots and dialed the numbers again.

"Please Cordell, one of y'all please answer this phone. My baby needs y'all," she said praying that someone would pick up. When no one picked up, she felt like throwing the phone against the wall, but she had to get her baby some help. So, she tried the numbers again.

Cordell and Ty-chelle were in the shower, they had just finished making love. She jumped out of the shower and ran over to the toilet and started throwing up.

"Baby what's wrong?" Cordell asked with concern.

"I don't know, lately I've been feeling really sick and I was supposed to come on last week and I didn't. At first, I thought it was just a change in my cycle, but now I don't know," she said looking at him trying to read his reaction.

"You know what, I've been throwing up myself. I thought it was something I ate. Maybe we should make an appointment for the doctor on Monday?"

"Yeah, I think I need to do that," Ty-chelle said. "What if I'm pregnant?"

"Then I'm going to be a daddy," Cordell said and held her close to him.

"What about your football and college?" she mumbled.

"The school ain't nothing but three hours away. I can come home on the weekends in the off season. And during the season, you could come up there."

"I love you baby!" she said moving even closer to him.

"I love you too!" he said allowing her to get closer.

They stood there holding each other, letting the warm water flow over their bodies. They dried each other off and went to the bed where he laid her down. He moved her hair from her face and kissed her, and they cuddled some more.

She pulled back a little and looked him in his eyes. "Cordell, promise me you'll never leave me," she said with a single tear in the corner of her eye.

He wiped the tear away and smiled at her. "Baby, as long as you respect our relationship and stay completely faithful to me, I promise I will never leave you."

She threw her arms around him again. "I love you so much for that."

"Then we'll be together forever," he said and kissed her on the neck.

"I like the sound of that. Forever."

They made love again, this time more passionately and then took another shower. "We're not getting on the bed this time," Cordell said smiling with love for his girl. Ty-chelle heard her phone beep, indicating she had a message.

Rome fired his last shot and didn't know what to do. He tried to think of something fast, but he couldn't think straight. "Damn, I can't believe I let these niggas catch me slipping and fucking with this bitch!" he thought to himself.

Capone, counting the shots, knew Tyrone had fired six shots, but he didn't know if he had anymore. Rome was known for the nickel plated .357 he carried, and Capone doubted he had extra bullets because he was not expecting this.

He motioned for one of his boys to go in, but you could see Bruno was reluctant. "He's going to pick me off just like he did J-Rock," Bruno said.

"He ain't got no more bullets," Capone said, not knowing for sure, but trying to ease Bruno's fear. Rome heard the man coming up the steps and didn't know what to do. He didn't have any more bullets and he knew the man was armed. He looked at the window and figured it was his only hope.

He told Karen to get under the bed then he went to the window and stepped out onto the roof.

As Rome was climbing out the window, Bruno reached the top of the steps. He saw Tyrone on the roof. "He's climbing out the window in the back!" he yelled down the steps. Everybody took off to the back of the house. Just as Rome jumped off the roof, Capone and some of his crew reached the back of the house. Rome took off, running for his life.

Ty-chelle reached down and grabbed her phone. She saw 20 missed calls, all from Karen. "Damn baby, Karen done called me 20 times."

"They probably bored trying to see what we're doing. Call them back."

Ty-chelle dialed the number and Karen picked up with panic in her voice. Ty-chelle heard the gun shots. "Karen what the fuck is going on?" she yelled into the phone.

"Oh my God! Oh my God! Rome!" Karen screamed, then ran to the window with the phone in her hand. She saw Rome laying in the grass motionless and Capone and his crew running off.

Cordell grabbed the phone out of Ty-chelle's hand. "Let me talk to Rome!" he yelled.

Karen was crying. "He's dead, Cordell, he's dead. He's lying in my backyard dead," she said into the phone.

"Quit playing with me Karen!" Cordell said, knowing that what she was saying could be true. Ty-chelle told him about the gunshots she heard. "Karen, please put Rome on the phone. This ain't funny. Please put him on the phone," he said again and again as tears began to flow from his eyes.

He let the phone drop to the floor as he went on his knees, his friend was really gone, and his tears started flowing even harder. "I told him to be careful. Why didn't he listen to me?" he said as he began hitting the floor with his fists. Ty-chelle grabbed him and pulled him to her chest as the tears ran down her cheeks onto the top of his head. "Why, Ty-chelle? Why didn't he just listen to me?" Cordell cried. She just held him, not saying a word, because she didn't have an answer and she knew that he wasn't really looking for one. She rocked him as if he were a baby, which in her eyes, he was. He was her baby and he was hurting.

CHAPTER 6

Rome's wake was at his church. So many people showed up to pay their respects. It almost looked like a block party. People from other crews called a truce and showed their respects. The police's presence was not overlooked because they were everywhere. A couple of correctional officers, who had escorted Rome's twin brother to the wake, were inside the church.

Cordell walked up to Rome's casket and saw his partner laying there looking like he was just sleeping. He noticed all the pictures and bandanas representing his set and many others laid there nicely. Tears formed in his eyes as he grabbed his partners hand and promised him on his word that he would find Capone and make him pay for this. "I love you my nigga!" he said, then headed for the door.

He heard someone call his name. He turned around and saw Karen running up to him. She had tears in her eyes and looked like she had not slept in a week. When she reached him, she tried to put her arms around him. "I'm sorry," she said. He looked at her, then spit in her face. "You're the reason he's dead. If I wouldn't have never turned him on to your trifling ass he wouldn't be dead," he said as he turned and walked off.

The people who saw this couldn't believe what they just witnessed, even Ty-chelle was in shock. This was not the Cordell they knew. The one they knew would never disrespect a woman like that, no matter what she had done. This person they saw was filled with anger and hate.

Ty-chelle walked up to her friend Karen and put her arms around her as Karen stared at the door in disbelief, long after Cordell was gone. "Are you okay, girl?" Ty-chelle asked. "I've never seen him act like that."

Karen laid her head on Ty-chelle's shoulder and began to cry uncontrollably. "He's right Ty-chelle, it's all my fault. If Cordell didn't introduce him to me he wouldn't be dead," she said, holding on to Ty-chelle tightly.

"Karen, it's not your fault. You didn't pull the trigger. Capone did and one day he is going to get what is coming to him. Rome's crew will make sure of that."

"If he didn't come to see me none of this would've happened. And now Cordell hates me."

"Don't worry about Cordell, he's hurting right now. Rome was like a brother to him. When he calms down, he'll see you're not to blame, but Capone is, and I'll make sure of that," Ty-chelle said, feeling sorry for her friend and could only imagine what she was going through.

That night as he was lying in bed with Ty-chelle, looking up at the ceiling, he felt bad for the way that he treated Karen and knew deep in his heart it was not her fault. He knew who was to be blamed: Capone, and he was going to pay for what had happened.

Ty-chelle looked up at him and could see the sadness in his eyes. She found out a couple of days ago, that she was pregnant, but she did not want to tell him because of all the things that was going on. She decided to tell him now, hoping that it would cheer him up, but when he didn't say anything, she understood and just held him tight.

Every night with the .38 Rome had given him, Cordell went out by himself searching for Capone. He would not stop until he found him and kept his word to his friend. Football, college and their unborn child was the furthest thing from his mind. Once he got Capone, he could focus on all that other stuff again. Right now, his only concern was finding Capone.

One night, he was out at the game room when Que, one of Rome's crew members came over to him. "My nigga, I know this nigga who knows exactly where Capone is hiding out." Cordell turned to him with rage in his eyes, "Where?" he asked coldly.

"My cousin fuck with this dude name Doe Boy, who's getting his money on the southside. He said he's got a partner named Leo whose sister could set that nigga up for us."

"Nah, I don't want her involved cause I'm murdering everything in sight. I just want to know where he is."

"I'll get with Doe boy and Leo and bring them by here."
"How soon can you do it?" Cordell asked.
"Tonight, about 9:00," Que answered.
"I'll be here."

For the first time in a month, Cordell could finally taste revenge and he was not going to let it slip away. He went home, got his .38 from under his bed and loaded it. He went in his closet, got some more bullets and put them on the bed. "They ain't going to catch me without no bullets like they did my nigga."

He grabbed a pair of black sweats and a black hooded sweatshirt, then he got out his black tims. He changed clothes, put the bullets in his pocket and sat on the bed, getting his mind together. Just like he used to do before big games. At ten minutes to 9, he headed for the game room. Que, Doe Boy and Leo were already there waiting on him. When he came in, he received the shock of his life. Doe Boy was Norm who played football with him and Leo was his best friend at one time.

"Man, Que, why didn't you tell me that it was Cordell Jenkins that is after Capone?" asked Doe.

"Shit, I didn't want to give out the niggas name in case something went wrong," said Que.

"What's up Norm? Leo? What y'all into? Whatever it is, it's treating y'all right," Cordell said, admiring their clothes and jewelry.

"Yeah, life has been alright, everybody didn't have big scholarship offers like you did," Leo said playfully, jabbing Cordell in his gut.

"So, what's up? Where this nigga been hiding?" Cordell finally asked impatiently.

"He kicks it with this little chick my sister be hanging with. One day I heard my sister talking about this nigga Capone be beating up on her friend. So, I asked her about him, and she said he some crib nigga off Maple, who's trying to lay low for a minute. Immediately, I knew who it was and got in touch with my nigga Que," said Leo, nodding his head in Que's direction.

"Your sister or her friend ain't going to be there, are they?" asked Cordell. "Cause I ain't trying to leave no witnesses!"

"I can do one better," Leo said, then reached in his pocket and gave Cordell a key. "They are going to be at the club around 12. He should be there by himself."

"Thanks, my nigga, I owe you one," said Cordell, sucking his teeth.

"You don't owe me shit. If you want, I'll roll with you cause Rome was a solid nigga," Leo said.

"Shit, I'll roll too," Norm, or Doe Boy as he now calls himself said, looking at Cordell for a response.

"I appreciate that my nigga's, but I got to do this myself," he said.

"Watch yourself," Que said as he and the fellas left the game room.

Cordell looked at the key in his hand and thought about his partner, Tyrone. "I promised you on my word that I was going to get this nigga and you know that I never break my word. He dies tonight."

He put the key in his pocket and walked to the house and waited. At ten minutes to one, he checked the gun again, put on his gloves and headed out the house to his car. "Capone, your ass is mine tonight and nothing in this world is going to save you, not even Jesus himself." He started the car and got on his way.

CHAPTER 7

Cordell pulled up in front of the house before the one Leo had told him Capone was hiding at. It was the last one on the block, at the end of a dead-end street. One way in and one way out. All the lights were out. He checked the windows and doorways of the other houses on the street to make sure no one was in them. He backed down the street and got out of the car.

As he walked down the street, he checked the houses again, only one of them had a light on and it was toward the back of the house. He eased up to the house where Capone was staying and put his ear to the door. He didn't hear anything. He took the gun from his pocket and unlocked the door with the key.

He turned the knob and the door slowly opened, he walked in very cautiously. It was dark, but he could see a light in the bedroom. With the gun raised, he slowly eased his way toward the opened door and saw Capone laying on the bed watching tv.

Capone could feel someone watching him. He looked out of the corner of his eye and saw what he thought was a shadow. He reached for his gun on the dresser. As soon as Capone moved, Cordell pushed the door up and unloaded the .38 into his body. He was dead before he hit the floor.

Cordell looked at Capone's lifeless body, loaded up the gun a second time and put six more bullets in his already dead body. "That's for me," he said as he ran out of the house.

He was driving down the street and he could still feel the rush from the reality of what he just did. He remembered how it felt when Tyrone first gave him the gun, how powerful he felt. Now that he had used it to murder a man, he felt even more powerful. He remembered what Rome said. "If you ever use it, throw it away." He rode through the park to make sure no police were hiding in the cut trying to catch somebody fucking. On the second trip around, he pulled over, got out and ran through the wooded area along the bank of the river in the park, and threw the gun as far as he could into the river.

If a policeman was at his car when he got back or was riding through and decided to stop him, he'd just say that he had to piss. All they would do is give him a ticket; it would be better than a murder rap. He got back in his car, picked up his cellphone and called Que, who was at the club with Leo and Doe. He told Que that Capone was no longer a part of this world and that he would meet them at the club.

He pulled up at his house, sat in the car for a second and thought about his friend. Then he looked up at the sky. "My word is my bond nigga." He got out of the car, wiped the tears from his eyes and went into the house.

Ty-chelle was asleep when he came in, he looked down at her and rubbed her belly, hoping not to wake her. He kissed her on her forehead then took off his clothes and got in the shower. "I'll call Tre tomorrow and get another gun," he said to himself. He washed off the dirt from the night, put on a fresh fit and met Que, Doe and Leo at the club. They wanted to know all the details, but Cordell didn't think it was appropriate. Plus, the less anybody knows, the safer he would be.

Weeks had passed since Capone's murder and the police still didn't have any suspects. Only three people knew who done it and Cordell wasn't worried about none of them. Que was loyal to Rome and grateful Cordell did the dirty work cause he had witnesses that saw him at the club around the time of the murder.

Leo always could be trusted by him and Norm. Well, Doe Boy was a true soldier himself and gained a lot from Capone's murder because he was able to slide in his hood and take over the drug game.

The next morning Cordell's phone rang. "Hello," he said, still asleep.

"What's up Killer?" said Doe, "What you got up for the day?"

"What time is it?" Cordell asked, rubbing sleep from his eyes.

"Nigga it's 10:00, get your ass up out of bed. Me and Leo coming to scoop you in about 40 minutes."

"Alright, I'll be ready," Cordell said, and he got up and took a shower.

Ty-chelle came in the bathroom while he was brushing his teeth. Her stomach was starting to look like a beach ball. She was still half sleep when she sat down on the toilet to pee. "Where you going?" she asked.

"Leo and Doe's getting ready to come and get me, they want to kick it for a while."

"At 10 in the morning?" she said, raising her eyebrows.

"Baby, you know how them niggas are, they don't never sleep," he said, trying to ease the tension.

"Don't get yourself in no trouble messing with them fools," she said, rolling her eyes at him.

"I won't," he said, kissed her and went downstairs. Doe pulled up with Leo on the passenger side and honked. "I told this nigga we would be here in about 40 minutes."

"He probably got to ask Ty-chelle if he could come out and play with us," said Leo. They both started laughing.

"Yeah, she be on his ass. I don't know why the niggas as faithful as a damn mutt," Doe said.

"That nigga's pussy whipped for sure, but Ty-chelle is a bad motherfucker," Leo added.

"Pretty or not, I'm not going to be stuck under no bitch all motherfucking day and I'm sure in hell, ain't going to let one tell me when and where I can go," Doe stated matter of factly.

"I know that's right," Leo said.

Five minutes later, Cordell came out of the house and got in the car. "My fault, I couldn't find my phone," he said, holding his phone in the air.

"Your woman probably hid that motherfucker, knowing you ain't going to leave without it," said Doe, as he pulled away.

"So, what's up, what are we getting into this morning?" asked Cordell, trying to change the subject about Ty-chelle controlling him.

"Same shit we get into every morning, getting fucked up and making some money," Leo said.

"What's really good Cordell, you trying to get some money or are you trying to be a killer?" asked Doe, looking through the rear-view mirror at Cordell.

"It ain't like that! I gave Rome my word that I was going to get that nigga and under no circumstances do I break my word," said Cordell.

"That's what I respect about you Cordell, you are a loyal motherfucker and we want you to get down with us and get some of this paper," Doe said trying to read Cordell's expression through the rear view.

"What y'all working with?" he asked.

"Right now, about a brick, but Doe got this connect in Miami and we are thinking about making a trip real soon," Leo said.

"My nigga said, if I come there, I can get them real cheap, but a nigga hate traveling on that highway," said Doe.

"Let me think about it," said Cordell. "I can use a little extra money, you know Ty-chelle's getting ready to have a baby."

"I heard about that. Congratulations," said Doe. They rode and kicked it for the rest of the day.

That night, they went to the club and Cordell thought about what Doe and Leo had offered; the means to provide for his unborn child and its mother. "I ain't never dealt drugs before, but if these two fools can do it, I know I can," he said to himself as he looked out of the window.

A month later, Doe and Leo hopped on a plane to Miami. They were excited because for the first time in their lives they had a real connect. In Louisville, bricks were going for 28 to 30 thousand dollars a piece and Miguel who was a Cuban said he could give it to them for 14 thousand a piece. All they had to do was come to Miami to get them.

That was easier said than done because coming through the turnpike out of Florida was a motherfucker and a nigga would need all the luck they could get. At 14 thousand a piece, it was worth the chance, cause if they made it, they were rich.

Doe remembered when he first met Miguel, he was in a club in Atlanta. he was at the bar ordering a drink when Miguel pulled up beside him. Right off, Doe knew he was important by the jewels he had on, even though it was just a watch and a pinky ring. He knew they cost him a grip because of all the diamonds.

Miguel looked at Doe and saw how he was admiring his ring. "You like that?" Miguel asked. Shocked that he was caught like a deer in headlights, he became speechless. "Huh?" was all he managed to say.

"I asked if you like my ring?"

"Oh, hell yeah! I know it cost you a grip," said Doe.

"My friend, it only cost pocket change," he said. "I'm Miguel."

"I'm Norm, but everybody calls me Doe."

"Doe, huh?" asked Miguel. "Where are you from Doe?"

"I'm from Louisville, Kentucky."

"I heard about that place. A couple of my friends do a little business up that way."

"What kind of business they do?" asked Doe, already knowing the answer, but wanting to see where Miguel's head was.

"Let's just say, the kind of business they do, they could afford 100 of these," he said wiggling his pinky fingers.

"I see," Doe replied, taking a sip of his drink.

"Let me ask you a question, how much are they paying in Louisville for kilos?" asked Miguel, watching Doe's expression.

Stunned by Miguel's forwardness, Doe did not know what to say. For the first time, he was starting to wonder if the guy sitting next to him was the police.

"What do you mean?" Doe responded.

"Listen Doe, I'm not the police. I could tell by your expression you're starting to wonder," Miguel said. "Look, here's my card. I can give you a kilo for 14 thousand a piece. I happen to know from my associates in Louisville, they go for 30 thousand and I want some of that business."

"Why me? How do you know that I'm not the police?" Doe asked.

"My friend, I'm a good judge of character and I trust my instincts. When you are ready, give me a call You have my number." He got up, extended his hand to Doe, shook it and made his exit.

"And that was just the luck of picking the right seat," Doe said to himself as he looked out of the window of the plane. He was now on his way to Miami to pick up 3 kilos.

When they got back in a couple of days, if they're lucky, him, Leo and Cordell were going to be making more money than any of them has ever seen.

Doe looked over at Leo as he slept. "How can that nigga sleep at a time like this? This plane could fall out of the sky or something, or some motherfucking terrorists could take over this motherfucker, and he's asleep!" he thought to himself and elbowed Leo in his side, making it look like an accident.

"What's up, we there?" Leo asked, looking around the plane.

CHAPTER 8

For the next few months, Cordell, Doe and Leo were getting money. It was more money than Cordell had ever made in his life. He was buying his unborn child—which they found out was a girl—all kinds of things. Him and Ty-chelle were sporting all the latest gear.

They were sitting in the park on a Sunday evening, watching all that Louisville had to offer, as far as the streets are concerned. Everybody who was anybody was in the park. This is where they could show their status. All the ballers with their nice jewels and freshly washed cars came through, All the pretenders with their fake jewelry and pocket full of ones with 50's or 100's on top. Then there were the women chasing both groups.

"I told you Cordell, this is the life baby," Doe said. "You could have any bitch out here you want just because they know you got paper."

"Let me remind you, in case you forgot; I could have any woman I wanted before I started getting paper," Cordell stated.

"My fault, I forgot, Mr. Football Star," Doe said, laughing loudly.

"Let me ask you something now that things done died down," Leo said. "They said Capone was shot twelve times. Nigga, you wanted to make sure that nigga was dead, huh?"

"Man, that nigga killed my partner over a bitch, I couldn't let that nigga breathe. What kind of friend would I have been if that nigga was still walking the streets and my nigga was in the ground?"

"You know Dino and the rest of his crew are trying to find out who actually done that shit. They know it was one of Tyrone's people. They just don't know which one, and they feel that bitch set him up. The police said it wasn't no forced entry," Leo stated.

"Fuck Dino and whoever else! That nigga Capone started this shit and if they don't like what happened to the nigga, they can get it too!" Cordell said, meaning every word. "I gave Tyrone my word that I was going to get that bitch nigga and I never break my word. Never!"

He went off in his own little world, Doe and Leo knew this by the blank look that came over his face, and they didn't want to disturb him. So, they just turned around and enjoyed the cycle of the streets, as they were facing that direction.

It started getting dark and everyone was starting to leave the park. The Sunday routine was, come to the park, go home, change clothes and hit Club 537, just to see the same people you just saw at the park.

"Think Ty-chelle will let you roll to the club with us tonight?" Doe asked, looking over the seat at Cordell.

"I don't have to ask for permission to do shit. I wear the motherfucking pants in that household!" stated Cordell.

"Alright nigga, whatever you say," Doe said as he turned and started the car.

That night at the club, it was just like it always was; everybody you saw at the park at every damn club you go to, was there. The only difference were the clothes they were wearing.

Cordell looked around as he got out of the car. "Damn, I'm tired of seeing the same people everywhere I go," he said to himself.

A group of girls walking pass called his attention. "How you are doing Cordell?" one of the girls said with a smile on her face that let him know if he wanted to fuck her right there, he could.

He remembered the girl's name was LaShonda. She went to Western or was it Central, he couldn't remember. He had met her at one of the schools during a girls' basketball game and remembered her name and face.

"I'm doing okay, how about yourself?" he asked, trying to be polite.

"I'll be doing a lot better if you save me a dance tonight," she said fluttering her long artificial lashes, while the other girls giggled.

"I'll see what I can do," said Cordell as he turned to face his boys. See, LaShonda wasn't his type. He remembered her as being a little too willing that night at the game and one thing he loved was a challenge.

Leo, on the other hand, didn't care, he would fuck anything with a slit in the middle. "Hey sweetheart!" he called after LaShonda. She stopped and turned around. "If he don't dance with you, I sure will," he said.

LaShonda, liking the attention, as most of the females out here do, gave him a smile with her eyes still on Cordell. "We'll see," was all she said, then turned to catch up with her friends.

"Damn Cordell, you turned that down? Shorty was fine, plus she was throwing herself at you," Leo said, looking at LaShonda and her friends as they crossed the street. "I know Ty-chelle got your ass pussy whipped now."

"Nah playboy, it ain't like that. Unlike you, I got a certain taste for women and she ain't my type." He didn't want to tell Leo that she was too easy. If he did, the poor girl wouldn't be able to enjoy herself all night cause he would be all on her.

When they entered the club, it was packed. A lot of people just play at the parking lot, but tonight, both the lot and the inside was sold out.

It was so dark, they couldn't see in all the corners, which is where most of the thugs look first, to see who they'll see. Most of the gangsta type niggas sit there, cause they didn't want to be seen or caught with their backs turned.

Cordell and his friends found a spot in the far-left corner furthest from the door, which he really didn't like. If some shit broke out, it's the furthest from the car where the guns were. However, it was the only corner spot unoccupied, so it would have to do.

He noticed LaShonda looking at him. "Damn, what is this chick, a bat? how the fuck she see me way over here?" he said to himself with his eyes still on her.

She was putting on a show for him, licking her lips and putting her finger in her mouth while staring at him the whole time. "These chicks are something else" he thought, "but I ain't going to lie, she got my dick hard."

He shook his head at her with a smile on his face and then turned away from her. Disappointed, she left the bar and walked onto the dance floor where Leo noticed her dancing by herself and shot to her. Frustrated, she rolled her eyes at Cordell and danced with Leo seductively, trying to make him jealous.

He laughed her off, then ordered a rum and coke with little ice. While he waited on his drink, he continued to observe his surroundings. He felt weird, like somebody was watching him. He turned to LaShonda and Leo on the dance floor, but she wasn't paying no attention to him. "Man, I'm just paranoid," he thought, dismissing the thought, and waited on his drink.

Finally, the waitress brought him his rum and coke, he took a sip; now he was comfortable, at least for the moment.

"Doe," he shouted over the music. Doe leaned over toward him. "That nigga Leo just ain't got no cut card, does he?"

Doe turned to look at the dance floor, then turned back to Cordell, "That nigga is pitiful, you should have seen that chick he took to the hotel the other night. Cold monster!" Doe said with a chuckle. Cordell shook his head and continued looking around the club.

Dino sat in the opposite corner, watching Cordell. He could see him because of the light from the bathroom, although it was barely lit, it was enough.

He saw Cordell looking around the room trying to see who was all in the club, but he knew he couldn't see him. "I know that nigga had something to do with Capone's murder, him and Tyrone were too close. Them two bitch niggas with him probably helped. I know Leo's sister hangs with that hoe, Sharon. And I still think she set him up," he thought, and then decided on his next move.

"Yo, Snaps, how many guns we got in the car?" Dino asked.

"I think about four or five. Why, what's up?"

"Nigga you don't know how many guns you put up?"

"Man, Rod packed the guns tonight, Dino!" replied Snaps.

"Well, you need to find Rod and find out cause I got a feeling we going to have to murder some niggas tonight."

Snaps got up from the table and went to look for Rod and prayed that something popped up, because if there is one thing Snaps liked, it was drama.

Cordell saw that crazy nigga Snaps, one of Capones boys, looking around the club, like he was in a hurry to find somebody. He knew if Snaps was in here, so was Dino, cause Dino wouldn't go nowhere without his number one trigger man.

"Doe," Cordell yelled over the music, "I got a bad feeling we going to have some problems tonight."

"Why you say that?"

"I just saw that nigga Snaps and I know that Dino ain't too far behind."

"Fuck it! It is what it is," stated Doe. "Where the fuck is Leo? That nigga's always somewhere chasing some pussy."

While Cordell was looking through the crowd for Leo, he spotted Snaps and Rod walking fast to the corner on the opposite side of the room. He followed them with his eyes and when they took a seat, he saw Dino and he was looking directly at him.

They locked eyes and at that moment he knew what time it was, and there was no doubt in his mind that Dino thought he murdered his partner and he wasn't going to let him walk out of here alive.

He told Doe he'd meet them outside, to give him his keys. Doe gave him the keys without saying a word. "Find Leo and get outside as soon as possible," Cordell said.

When Cordell got up and headed for the door, Dino knew where he was going. He motioned for his boys to come on and they all left the club.

Cordell opened the trunk and removed a .44 and a .38 from under the spare tire. He saw Dino and his crew running to their car. They jumped in and pulled off.

Doe and Leo were coming across the street looking in the direction of the speeding car, as it turned the corner at the far end of the block. Leo noticed the guns in Cordell's hand. "What's up?" he asked, but before another word could be spoken, there was a loud sound of screeching tires, and then, pop! pop! pop! pop! pop!

Cordell pulled the .44 and the .38 and fired, cha! cha! cha! boom! boom! boom! at the speeding car. When he turned around, he saw Doe laying up against the car with blood gushing out of his stomach and shoulder.

He bent down next to his friend. "Hold on my nigga, don't you die on me," he said.

"Them niggas came from out of nowhere," said Doe.

"I know my nigga, just try not to talk," Cordell said with tears rolling down his face. "Not again!" he thought.

He knew the ambulance would take forever to get there, especially with the traffic the way it was, so they threw Doe in the car and rode down a one-way street toward the traffic and cars moved out of their way. The hospital was right down the street, hopefully they could make it without the police pulling them over. Cordell had it in his mind that if they did, he wasn't going to stop until they got to the hospital.

At the hospital, the police asked Cordell if he knew who did the shooting and he had done lied saying he didn't know. He said he didn't believe the bullets were meant for his friend, which wasn't a lie. Cordell knew they were meant for him and that is what hurt more than anything.

The officer told him if he hears anything to let him know. He told him he would, but that was another lie, because Cordell lives by the code of the streets: "it happened in the street, we deal with it in the streets," and that's exactly what he was going to do.

• • •

As they sped down the long stretch of road, Dino asked Snaps, "Did you get Cordell?"

"I don't know if it was him, but I know that I hit somebody cause I saw them fall."

"Maybe we should ride back through?" said Rod.

"Nah, that wouldn't be a good idea. For one, they will be waiting on us and the police might be there by now," Dino said, "If we missed him, we'll get another chance." Little did they know that would be their last chance. Cordell was out for blood and he wasn't going to rest until he got it and kept his word to Doe.

Dino pulled up in front of the clubhouse, they all got out and went inside. They cleaned the fingerprints off the guns so they could get rid of them. The last thing they were worried about was the police, cause they knew Cordell wasn't a rat. He lived by the code of the street, even though he wasn't a real street nigga.

The murder of Tyrone forced Cordell into this life and now he was devoted to it. Dino knew this, because when he looked into his eyes at the club tonight. He saw the eyes of a cold-blooded killer. At that moment he knew for a fact that Cordell was responsible for Capone's murder, and that made him dangerous.

He wanted to take him out, and he hoped like hell they did, but deep inside he knew they missed. Sooner or later he was going to come after him if they indeed missed, and this worried him.

He wasn't going to underestimate him like Capone did, and he knew he had to move fast. If he got to Capone, getting to him would be easy. He wasn't the type to go into hiding. He laid his head against the back of the chair and thought about his next move. First, he had to find out if it was Cordell who fell, which would make it a little easier because he was wounded. However, if it wasn't, he knew life would become difficult for him, and he would have to watch his back.

"Damn, I should've done that shit differently and made sure I got that nigga," he said as he slammed his fist into the arm of the chair.

CHAPTER 9

The doctor came to the waiting room where Doe's mother, Cordell, Leo and a few other family members were sitting, hoping for the best. He said Doe would live, and everyone sighed with relief, especially Cordell. He knew he would be sedated for a few days in the Intensive Care Unit, so there was no need visiting him.

It would give him a chance to think and figure out his next move, hopefully, by the time by the time Doe comes around, he'll have some good news for him. Hopefully, he'll be able to tell Doe that he kept his word and that Dino and Snaps are with Capone in hell.

When he got home, Ty-chelle was up waiting on him. He had called her from the hospital and told her what had happened and she had already run his bath water. He got in, added a little hotter water and closed his eyes as he laid back in the tub.

"Damn, these niggas tried to kill me. They must've figured out that I killed Capone. It ain't going to stop until one of us is dead and I don't plan on it being me," he thought.

He dried off and went and laid down across the bed. Ty-chelle crawled up next to him, rubbing his back with her hand. "You okay baby?" she finally said as she laid her head on his back and kissed his shoulder.

"Yeah, I'm okay. Just a little shocked, I guess."

"Is Doe okay?"

"The doctor said he was going to make it. It will be a few days before he'll be able to talk to visitors."

She slid down beside him and wrapped her arms around him as she kissed the side of his head. "I love you Cordell," she said.

"I love you too," he said, and they fell asleep in each other's arms.

The next morning, Cordell went to the hospital to see Doe. He was completely out of it, high off the medication they had given him. He was told the police had been up there several times, he just hoped Doe didn't give them Dino's without realizing it.

He looked down at his friend who tried to speak, but he couldn't understand what he was trying to say.

"Man, don't try to talk," Cordell said, very concerned about his partner. "I'm just here to check on you."

Doe tried to speak again and this time he understood a little of it.

"Nah, I haven't got them yet. But I gave you my word, and if it's the last thing I do on this earth, I'm going to get them," said Cordell in Doe's ear, not knowing who might be listening.

Doe managed to give him a smile knowing his dog had his back. It reminded him of their football days when Cordell used to catch up with him and run his laps with him after he had already ran his. He knew Cordell was a true friend and him laying in this bed fighting for his life wouldn't go unpunished. Dino and Snaps will pay, and he was certain of that. After all, Cordell gave him his word and he never breaks that.

"They are having a party this weekend and trust me, you're going to read about it. It's going to be the last party either of them niggas go to until their funerals. And hopefully, that nigga Rod too," he said still close in Doe's ear. "I'm going to get out of here and let you get some rest. I'll be back up here this weekend. Love ya, my nigga!"

Doe squeezed his hand to let him know that he loved him too. Cordell got up, looked down at his friend one more time and walked out the door with tears in his eyes. He knew in his heart that it was his fault Doe was laying in that bed and that thought angered him. "Dino, I hope you made your peace with God cause this is your last few days on the fucking earth," Cordell said to himself as he walked out of the hospital, wiping his face with the sleeve of his shirt.

Saturday night, Dino and his crew were having a birthday party for someone. It was one of those backyard parties in the hood. Crap ass music, very little lighting and a whole lot of drinks.

Leo parked the stolen car at the end of the block on the corner. Cordell got out of the car wearing his usual murder gear, black hoodie, black sweats and black tims. The best part about it is that it didn't make him stand out, because, that is every hood niggas outfit. He checked his guns, he had the .44 and .38 with him. He knew this was a bold move, and Leo told him he was crazy, but he figured this was the only way. He might not get another chance and he damn sure wasn't going to wait until they came after him again. Plus, he wanted that nigga Dino so bad it didn't matter.

His only fear was that someone would recognize him before he got off a shot, or became suspicious and warned someone. He doubted the last part because he knew everybody would be drunk, which was why he waited so late.

"Fuck it!" he said, throwing the hood over his head and walked like he was one of the drunk party goers. He walked right into the middle of the back yard. Right into the middle of the crew whose leader he murdered a few months ago. Right into the middle of the crew whose current leader he was going to murder tonight.

He posted up on the fence looking for Dino or Snaps, but he didn't see either of them. Maybe they were in the house, but it was to much light in there and would be to risky. He got a couple of stares, but nothing to alarm him. He kept his fingers on the trigger of the guns in the pocket of the hoodie just in case he had to shoot his way out.

"Where are these bitch niggas at?" he said to himself. He saw Rod, but he didn't want him, not yet anyway.

He knew he couldn't wait so much longer. "I'll give these niggas a few more minutes. I know they're here. They got to be." After a few minutes he decided to leave. Frustrated, he got back into the car.

"What happened? I was waiting to hear gunshots," Leo said.

"Them niggas ain't even in that motherfucker," said Cordell.

"Where to now?"

"Man, just drive around, these niggas' hood, they got to be somewhere."

Just when Leo was pulling off Cordell spotted what he thought was Dino and Snaps, walking with two females.

"Ease up on them niggas there, it might be them," said Cordell, trying to get a better look. Leo pulled up and you could hear the group laughing. Cordell pulled his hood over his head. "It's a damn shame these niggas are so comfortable in their own hood, they don't pay attention to shit. Now they are getting ready to die for it," he thought.

"Stop right here," he told Leo. He got out of the car and eased up behind the group. "What's up cuz?"

Snaps was the first to turn around to what he thought was a fellow member of his crew, but instead, got a .38 shell to the head. Before Dino could do anything, Cordell blew the back of his head out with the .44. He looked at the screaming girls, "Y'all have a nice night." Then he walked back to the waiting car as if nothing happened.

Leo watched everything in shock, put the car in drive and pulled off. "You are a crazy motherfucker," he said. "I never want to get on your bad side."

Cordell laid back and they drove in silence the rest of the way to their hood.

• • •

Rod and the rest of the crew heard the gunshots, they pulled their guns and ran towards the sound. By the time they got there, whoever did the shooting was gone. They saw Dino with the whole back of his head blown completely out. His brains and pieces of his skull were all over the pavement. It made some of the onlookers throw up. Snaps was laying in the grass with his eyes still open and a hole in his head.

The two girls who were with them were in shock, one of them could barely breathe. Her whole body was shaking and tears started to run from her eyes.

Rod couldn't believe what he was seeing. "Who did this?" he shouted at the girls.

"It looked like Cordell," one of the girls managed to say, "but he had on a hood and it was hard to tell, but I'm almost sure it was him."

One of the crew members said, "I saw a nigga in the party standing by the fence with a black hood on and I didn't know who he was."

"I know that nigga wasn't that bold to come up in our party," Rod said.

"Did he have on some black sweats and black tims?" the guy asked the girl.

"Yeah," was all she could say through the tears.

"I'll be damned!" Rod said, but what he was really thinking was, "I'm not fucking with this nigga if he is that motherfucking bold."

The police came, removed the bodies and got statements from everybody. They took Rod and the girls along with the guys inside the party down to the police station.

Before the crack of dawn, they had a suspect. Even though it was hard to believe, because the officer knew this name well. He worked some of the games at the school Cordell played for, a couple of years ago. He put out a warrant for the arrest of Cordell Jenkins, the ex-football star.

CHAPTER 10

Cordell and Ty-chelle were laying in the bed sleeping when the phone rang and woke him up.

"Hello," he said, still half asleep.

"What's up?" the voice on the other end cheerfully said.

"Who is this?" Cordell said, still not recognizing the voice.

"Nigga, it's Doe! You said I was going to read about it and I'll be damned if it isn't all over the news this morning."

"My word is bond." He forced a little smile.

"Dig this, they said they got a suspect, so you better lay low for a minute."

"Forreal!" Cordell exclaimed, finally waking all the way up. "You mean them bitch motherfuckers gave the police my name?"

"I don't know if they gave your name, but they got somebody's name. Just in case, chill out for a little while."

"Alright my nigga, good lookin." Cordell hung up the phone and thought about what to do next.

"Man, I can't believe these motherfuckers told on me. Shit, when they rode for me and shot Doe, I didn't say shit," he thought as he laid in the bed.

He reached over and woke Ty-chelle up. He told her she needed to get dressed, pack some clothes and go stay at her mother's house. She looked at him confused and asked him what was going on. He told her, "Just do what I tell you."

This was the first time he had ever talked to her like that and she intuitively knew something was very wrong.

"Cordell, what is going on baby?" she demanded to know.

"Baby look, some things have come up that I need to take care of and I don't want to be worrying about you, so baby please, just do as I've asked you."

"I'm not doing nothing until you tell me what the hell is going on!"

"Listen to me, damn it!" he said raising his voice, he knew this situation was stressing him out. If there was anybody in this world besides Doe and Leo that he knew he could trust, it was her, so he started from the beginning and told her everything.

"Now you see why I need you to go and stay with your mother? I don't know if Rod and his crew are coming for me or if the police are looking for me. Either way, I can't have you in the crossfire."

With tears forming in her eyes she said, "Why Cordell, why? I told you them niggas was going to get you in some trouble and you didn't listen to me."

"They didn't make me do anything I didn't want to do. I fucked up, Ty-chelle, and baby, all I can do is say that I'm sorry and hope they didn't give the police my name."

"Is that why you haven't called them schools back and stopped talking about playing football?" she asked, looking him directly in the eye.

"I've been so caught up in these streets that I forgot about school and football," he said, knowing she deserved the truth.

"Do you think them punk motherfuckers would have done the same for you? Just throw away their lives and dreams?" she said.

"I can't answer that question, but I honestly believe that if the shoe was on the other foot, they would have done the same." This was no lie. He really believed that Doe and Leo would've done the same for him and he trusted them with his life.

For the next few weeks, Cordell laid low. Doe got him a lawyer, even though he could have paid for his own. He wasn't stupid and put a lot of money to the side for rainy days, and this was a very rainy day.

The lawyer's name was Romone Scott. He was a black lawyer who had a lot of pull in the court system. He had gotten Doe out of so much shit, he didn't know where to begin the list.

The other attorneys thought he was crooked, and he was, but in a trial where the prosecutor or judge wouldn't take a bribe, he still handled his business and won most of the time, if not all of the time. For this reason, a lot of prosecutors didn't want to go up against him in a trial and were quick to offer plea deals.

"So, what's it looking like?" Cordell asked Mr. Scott while sitting across from him in his office.

"To tell you the truth Mr. Jenkins, it ain't looking good at all," replied Mr. Scott. "But if you can get to these witnesses and get them under control, we might be able to pull off a miracle."

"Shit, how can I get them under control when I don't know who the fuck they are. You said they have four? I know one of them is probably Rod, but who are the other three?"

"That's the problem," said Mr. Scott. "Until they arrest you and give us a motion of discovery, which would be about a month later, we won't know who they are."

"Basically, what you're saying is that I should turn myself in and let my people handle the witnesses?"

"It looks about the easiest way Cordell."

"Damn!" Cordell said and leaned back in the chair. He ain't never been to jail before and now his attorney wants him to volunteer. "I don't know about that one there Mr. Scott. I'm facing two bodies and they got witnesses."

"I understand where you're coming from, but this is the only way to fight it and with any luck, we'll get the right prosecutor or judge," said Mr. Scott.

"Let me think about it and see what my people say, and I'll get back with you."

"Okay Cordell, but trust me, this is the best way," Scott said and got up to shake hands with Cordell.

"I'll get back with you in a couple of days," Cordell said as he walked out of the door.

• • •

Over the next couple of days, Cordell spent as much time as possible with Ty-chelle during the day. At night, Cordell,

Doe and Leo searched for Rod and tried to find out who these other witnesses were.

They thought they had figured out who one of them was. Her name was Kim Brown. She was one of the girls with Dino and Snaps the night Cordell murdered them.

For some reason. they couldn't find her either, so they figured the information they got must have been true. Their only hope was her and Rod was somewhere hiding and not in protective custody.

This made it difficult for Cordell to turn himself in, because he hadn't taken care of the witnesses. Even though Doe and Leo promised him they would find them and it might be best if he was locked up when they did, he still thought twice about it.

He trusted his partners and knew they wouldn't let him down. So, two days later, with Romone Scott in tow, he turned himself in to the police.

The next morning, Cordell was escorted into the courtroom by four guards for his arraignment. When he entered, he saw all the lights from the news cameras. The whole courtroom was lit up like a football field. How ironic, was all Cordell thought. Through the lights he could see his mother, Ty-chelle, Doe and Leo on the first row and he smiled at them, which was a mistake in front of all the cameras. He was charged with two counts of first-degree murder and ordered to be held without bond. His attorney asked for a bond hearing and a date was set for a week later.

As he was escorted back out the courtroom by the four guards, he looked back and saw the tears in his mother's and Ty-chelle's eyes.

"I love you," Ty-chelle mouthed.

"I love you too," he mouthed too.

When he got back to his dorm, some of the guys that didn't know who he was, were now staring at him. They had seen the news and newspaper.

One of the guys gave him the paper. He grabbed it, opened it, and was taken aback by the headlines in big bold letters across the top: **SHATTERED DREAMS!** He began reading his own highlight reel.

> **Cordell Jenkins, the prominent football star, who had the potential to be one of the best athletes to ever come out of the state of Kentucky, is now being charged with two counts of First-Degree Murder in the shooting deaths of Dion Daniels and Samuel Smith, two local gang members. It is not known what drove the star to commit these horrific crimes.**

He couldn't read anymore. He threw the paper on the table and went to bed. he took his shoes off and laid down, looking up at the ceiling. He remembered the words Coach Kendricks said to him: "Son, you got the potential to be one of the best football players to ever come out of the state of Kentucky." And here it was again, under the title "Shattered Dreams."

He turned over and faced the wall cause he didn't want the other inmates to see his tears. For the first time, he realized what he lost and thought about the words again, "Shattered Dreams." That's exactly what he did when he walked off that field a year and a half ago, his dreams shattered.

One of the inmates in the dorm whom Cordell knew walked over to his bed. His name was Curt. He knew Tyrone and bout what happened, so he felt sympathy for Cordell. "You alright my nigga?" Curt asked him, hitting Cordell's bed with his hand.

Not even turning over to face the other man Cordell just simply said, "Shit happens."

"I feel that, but trust me, it ain't the end of the world and for the record, I would have done the same thing if they rode for me," Curt said.

Confused and wanting to know how Curt knew so much, he turned toward him. "What are you talking about my nigga?" Cordell asked, looking suspicious.

"I was at the club that night. I saw them gun for y'all and hit your partner," he said, "but you ain't got to worry about me, I ain't no rat."

"That's good to know," Cordell said and rolled back over, leaving Curt standing there, then he walked back out into the day room.

CHAPTER 11

Six months of back and forth to the courtroom was hell. Tychelle had a beautiful baby girl that she named Corchelle. She brought her to visit Cordell every day.

Doe and Leo had found the other three witnesses whose names were in the motion of discovery; Kim Brown was indeed one of them. They paid them to change their stories, but they couldn't find Rod.

All he needed was to make sure Rod didn't show up. Even though he didn't really see the shooting, but he could testify about the beef and the prosecutor might try to make something out of that. But without him the prosecutor wouldn't even consider a trial.

Four more months went on the same way; more court appearances, motions filed by his attorney and the prosecutor. Then, three weeks before trial, Mr. Scott came to Cordell with an offer from the prosecutor.

"Well Cordell, it seems some of the witnesses have changed their stories and now they are not so sure if it was you who did the shooting."

"I wonder what changed their minds?" Cordell said, smiling to himself.

"I don't know what did it," said Mr. Scott, knowing Cordell and his friends had something to do with it, but it would be unprofessional for him to acknowledge it and he didn't know who might be listening. "The prosecutor has offered you a deal for ten years on each count to run concurrent."

"Have you heard anything about Rodrick Anderson?" asked Cordell.

"It seems Mr. Anderson is put up somewhere and that's why I suggest you take this deal because it seems Mr. Anderson knows a lot more than what we thought, or the prosecutor is trying to make it seem that way."

"How long do I have to think about it?"

"Probably two weeks. The prosecutor needs to know something before the trial date. Mr. Jenkins, I don't think you're going to get a better offer than this for two murders."

"Yeah, I feel you," Cordell said as he got up from the table, shook Mr. Scott's hand and left.

That night, Ty-chelle came to visit, and Cordell told her about the deal. "Well baby, it seems I'm going to have to take it," he said.

"So, how long will you actually be gone?" she asked.

"They say you can serve out ten years in six years and six months. I'll go up for parole in four years, so, I'll have a chance to come home in three more years."

"Well, three years ain't too long, and you know I ain't going nowhere. I will bring the baby to see you every weekend," she promised.

"That's why I love you so much cause I knew I could trust you, and no matter what, I know you would have my back," Cordell said.

They sat and talked about some other issues and about how Cordell's mother was doing. Then it was time for her to leave and this was always the hardest part.

"I love you baby girl!" he said as he kissed his two fingers and put them up against the glass window.

"I love you too!" said Ty-chelle as she did the same.

Two weeks later Cordell took the deal as his mother, Ty-chelle, Doe and Leo watched from their seats in the courtroom.

When the Judge sentenced Cordell to serve ten years in the Department of Corrections, tears fell from his mother's eyes.

On the way to the fish tank, which is where they take all the inmates from county jails around the state of Kentucky to process them, Cordell had all kinds of thoughts going through his mind.

He had heard so many stories about prison and even though he knew a lot of them weren't true, he didn't know what to expect.

His aunt Brenda had written him during his ten months in jail and tried to prepare him as best as she could. She was in a women's prison and to her it was ten times worse than a men's.

She told him to give respect and you'll get it in return and if someone doesn't respect you, make him. If you can kill on the streets, you can kill in prison especially if a motherfucker fuck with you.

Her main rule was never ever tell the officers shit, no matter what they threaten you with, but he already knew that one, he lived by that code on the streets.

The rest of the way there, most of the other inmates were silent as well, thinking their own thoughts. There were a few who weren't first timers and they acted like they were going to a party.

The bus came to a stop in front of a long fence with barbwire across the top and in between this one and another one. There was a guard standing outside a big tower with a shotgun. Cordell wondered for the first time, what the hell he'd gotten himself into.

They were led shackled at the hands and feet into a large building with electronic doors. Once inside, they were unshackled and ordered to strip down to their birthday suits. Cordell had been naked in front of a lot of men in the locker rooms, but he felt degraded to have to get naked in this cold dull looking place. He felt like an animal.

After they were all naked, they sprayed them with bug spray and made them get in the shower, one after another without cleaning it.

Then they took all kinds of blood tests and gave them a series of shots. Once they were done, they were given blue uniforms that looked like doctor scrubs and then were led to dorms.

There were 36 beds on each side of the long wall. The bathroom was all the way at the back of the room. There was a T.V. up front and two phones. Each bed had a locker assigned to it where the inmate kept his belongings.

Cordell looked around and saw a couple of people that he knew, and they spoke. He made his bed and by the time that he finished some inmates had come in from the rec. His Bunkie came and introduced himself.

"What's up man, my name is Moody."

"What's up, I'm Cordell."

They became friends instantly, along with another guy named Chew and from then on, they were like the three amigos. Ironically, they all ended up getting shipped to the same place, which was pure luck. Their friendship grew and they got really tight. From there they would go on to form a clique called "B.B.C." The Black Billionaires Club. They would carry it to the streets.

CHAPTER 12

Moody was 5'7", dark skinned with long dreads. He wore a goatee, which he kept neat and trim, and he considered himself the Hugh Hefner of the hood.

He was a legend where he was from, which was a small county in Western Kentucky. His money was so long he could do a hundred years and never run out.

Chew was 6'2", brown complexion with a fade. He always rocked a full beard that seemed like he shaped up every day. He was from Louisville, same as Cordell. Even though they didn't know each other personally, they'd heard of one another.

Chew was quick to pop that pistol and didn't give a fuck about who it hit. Plus, his mouth was bad, so they kept little drama, but hey, what's prison without a little drama.

Every day you could find these three somewhere, kicking it, talking about what they were going to do when they hit the streets, which seemed like a long way off to them, but in all reality, it wasn't. And that's why they could still dream.

Chew had a little over 18 months left before he served out, Moody had 20 years, but his case was in front of the Supreme Court with a 99% chance of being overturned. The police done some fucked up shit, they broke in his house and stashed dope in different spots and then raided his house a few hours later. One of the cops came clean and told on the others, so he'll be out before Chew and Cordell.

There was another cat they played dominoes with. His name was "I was getting ready to" or "I almost Tyson." They called him this because every day he claimed he was getting ready to or he almost whooped somebody. Moody and Chew gave him the blues. Cordell thought that was the reason that he stopped coming around.

"Damn, this time seemed to have slowed down. This shit was moving faster than a motherfucker at the beginning," Cordell said to Chew and Moody.

"I know what you're saying," Moody said. "My shit been in the supreme court for 11 months now, and them motherfuckers still ain't brought my shit before the panel."

"Nigga, if I was you, I'll have my lawyer balling them stinking ass bitches every day," said Chew.

"Shit, I wish it was that easy my nigga, but unfortunately, these motherfuckers play by their own rules," Moody replied.

"Then they wonder why a motherfucker want to kill judges, police and prosecutors," Chew said.

"I tell you what, when I get out of this motherfucker I'm going to ball until I fall and then I'll hold court in the streets," said Cordell.

"Damn right!" Chew replied, and they all shook their heads in agreement.

It would be like this for the seven months. Then Moody was called to the caseworker's office and told he would be going home in a couple of days; all they were waiting on was the paperwork.

He came out and told Cordell and Chew the good news. They were sad that he was leaving, but happy that he was getting out of prison. They knew that he would start putting their plans in motion. A plan that would change their lives forever, they were sure of it.

Mail Call! The officer yelled out. "Jenkins!" He called Cordell's name twice. One was from Ty-chelle and the other was from Doe. He read Ty-chelle's letter first, then opened Doe's.

> Cordell,
> I pray that this letter finds you in the best of health, as well as in the happiest of spirits. I myself am doing well, considering the circumstances.
> I was hoping you would have called because you know that I hate writing. There has been an

unfortunate accident. My cousin, Miguel who lives in Miami was killed last week.

The family is messed up over this situation because a lot of the assets were in his name and now they can't be found.

This is causing a great strain on everyone involved because he controlled the family business. I remember you saying you had a friend who was about to get out who knows about the law and could possibly help.

If it wouldn't be a great deal of trouble, could you have him contact me and we could work out a reasonable price for his assistance.

I will be waiting to hear from you and I'm sorry for bringing this burden upon you.

Much Love,
Norm

Cordell put the letter down and evaluated its contents. The first part was easy. Miguel was Doe's connect down in Miami. He must've gotten killed last week and now Doe is shit out of luck as far as a connect goes. Now, he'll have to pay those high ass prices again.

"What did he mean the assets were in his name and now they can't find them?" This puzzled Cordell because he had no idea what Doe was trying to tell him.

He knew Doe sent the money to Miami and then him and Leo would fly down there and drive the dope back. Then it hit him. "He sent the money to Miguel and he got killed before he could get to Miami to pick up the work," he said to himself. "Now he wants me to hook him up with Moody when he gets out tomorrow."

Cordell had been writing Doe and Leo, telling them about the two niggas he met, Chew and Moody.

He told them about Moody getting his paper and about B.B.C. He also let them know to never write a letter about drugs or talk on the phone about it when he calls.

He wasn't worried about the letters he sends out because he knows they don't read them, but they read the ones coming in, as well as record your phone calls. That is why Doe wrote the letter the way that he did.

Cordell knew Doe was about his money and knew he could be trusted. His nigga took a loss and he was going to do everything he could to help him.

He hollered at Moody and put him up on the situation. Moody said as soon as he was straight, he would holler at Doe and help him out. Cordell gave him the number.

The next morning, he was released and immediately began building the status of B.B.C., while waiting on Cordell and Chew to join him.

After Moody was released, Cordell and Chew still kicked it every day. They would receive money orders and pictures from him and even talk to him on the phone often.

Tyson even started trying to come around them again. Since Moody was gone, he didn't have nobody to call him a doorknob or dummy, or so he thought. Chew was still giving it to him. Eventually, he stopped coming around again, which didn't hurt Cordell's or Chew's feelings.

Chew came in the dorm after leaving the phone area, which was in another building by itself one day and said to Cordell, "Cordell, Moody said to call him."

"What he hollering about, I got to finish ironing my clothes, wifey coming up in the morning with my shorty."

"He asked me if you got that bread that he sent you and those pictures of them stinking ass bitches? I told him I think you did."

"Nigga, why didn't you just tell him that I got them? You saw them."

"Shit, I didn't know for sure those came from him. You be getting pictures and shit from Doe and Leo's sorry asses too. I still for the life of me, don't know why you fuck with them lame ass niggas."

Chew knew Doe and Leo, but for some reason, never liked them, but Cordell never asked him why.

"Man, them niggas alright, they always kept it real with me and plus, they look out for me and wifey."

"Them niggas are lames and one day you're going to find out the hard way. I wish I would've killed that nigga Leo when I had the chance," Chew said, thinking back.

"Nigga, that's your problem, always wanting to kill a motherfucker," said Cordell.

"Motherfucker, look who's talking nigga, what you got, three bodies?"

"Damn nigga, what you trying to do, give a nigga some more time? I ain't got but two bodies?"

"Yeah, alright nigga, remember, I'm from the same hood as you are Jesse James," Chew said as they both started laughing.

Cordell finished ironing his clothes and then went and called Moody. He answered on the third ring. The operator went through the motions and they they were connected.

"What it do my nigga?" Moody said when Cordell clicked in.

"What's really good?" said Cordell.

"Shit is beautiful out here my nigga and I can't wait til you and Chew show."

"Chew should be showing real soon and I ain't got but a few more months," Cordell said.

"Look, dig this, I hollered at your man Doe and Leo. We kicked it for a minute and dude, I'm not feeling them, especially that cat Leo."

"Man, dude is alright, he just kind of weird and Doe gets his paper."

"I feel that, and I looked out real tough on the strength of you."

"I appreciate that my nigga and you'll see, them niggas alright," said Cordell.

"If you say so, but anyway, you get that paper I sent you, along with the pictures?"

"Yeah, I got them."

"Them was some thick bitches wasn't they?" Moody said.

"That one bitch in that red thong was a motherfucker," said Cordell.

"When you come home my nigga, I'll bring her to Louisville for you. In fact, I'll bring her with me to come and pick you up," Moody said.

"I don't think wifey's going to have that."

"You know that's right," Moody said. "If you need anything call me."

"Alright," Cordell said, and they hung up.

Cordell sat and thought for a minute. He didn't understand why his new friends didn't like his old ones. Especially Leo cause he and Leo was closer than him and Doe.

"Fuck it!" he said and picked up the phone to call Doe.

After what seemed like forever, Doe clicked in. "Damn nigga, about time you called," he said.

"I've been meaning to call you, but I've been busy trying to get this shit together so a nigga can be right when I step out of the motherfucker."

"All you got to do is get out of there, I'm going to make sure you're alright."

"I hear you my nigga. I talked to my people and they told me they took care of you," Cordell said.

"Yeah, that nigga there is a real nigga, plus, he talks highly of you and can't wait for you to come home."

"You don't find too many niggas like him," Cordell said.

"Can say that again," Doe said. "By the way, when are you coming home?"

"If everything goes right, I should be out of here in about three months."

"Damn! six years done passed that quick, it only seems like you've been gone about three years."

"Time has flew by, but trust me my nigga, it hasn't been fun," said Cordell.

"Well shit, since you on your way home, I might as well give you the real," Doe said not knowing if he should tell Cordell what he knows, but what kind of friend would he be if he didn't. "Look here my nigga," Doe started, "Ty-chelle been kicking it with this nigga named Aaron."

"What?!" Cordell shouted into the phone. "How long you been knowing this?" he calmed down and said.

"I found out about a month ago when I dropped off some money over there and he was there. I didn't think nothing of it at first, but then I started riding past and caught him over there a couple more times. So, I asked him, and he told me he didn't know about you, so I told him don't wake her up."

"Damn! I can't wait til that bitch come here tomorrow, I'm subject to get some more time."

"Nah homie, don't play your hand like that. I wouldn't let her know you know cause you know she still got some of your paper."

"You're right, but why didn't you tell me before now? I've been kissing that bitch and everything and no telling what the bitch was doing the night before she came up here."

"You my nigga, and I know you are going through enough shit dealing with the everyday life of being in prison. The last thing I wanted to do was put more stress on your plate."

"Dig that my nigga. I still wish you had told me sooner. That way I could've gotten my bread out of her hands. Let me get off here so I can go smoke a black before they close the yard."

"Alright, keep you head up and if yo need me you know how to reach me," Doe said before hanging up.

Cordell went to the smoke shack and fired up a black. "Damn, I can't believe Ty-chelle played me like that. I gave the girl my all and she go and cross me like that. I'm wondering where my daughter was while she was doing all this fucking around," he thought to himself.

He finished the black, then walked to his dorm.

Chew was at the microwave fixing something to eat when Cordell finally came back to the dorm.

"You caught him?" he said.

"Yeah, he had his girls' house phone transferred to his cell. He said we should be able to call straight to his cellphone on Monday."

"So, is that what was so important that the nigga had me run over here to have you call him? Shit, he could have just told me to tell you that."

"He also wanted to know if I got the pictures, since you didn't know, and he told me he hooked up with Doe and Leo on some business like I asked him to."

"Cordell, I know you didn't do that man? I know you did not hook him up with them lame ass niggas?"

"What you got against Doe and Leo?" Cordell finally asked.

"Them niggas are marks, plus, they are whores. I saw a nigga take Doe's shit and didn't even have a gun and he didn't do shit. I know they your dogs and all that, but I'm telling you now, that nigga Leo is going to be your downfall, mark my word," said Chew.

"I got so much other shit on my mind right now, I can't even think about that."

"What's going on my nigga?" Chew asked.

"When I got off the phone with Moody, I called Doe. He told me wifey been fucking around."

"Forreal? Do you think you can trust what that nigga say, I told you that he was a lame."

"That nigga ain't going to tell me no bullshit, plus, he pulled up on the nigga and the nigga told him, but said that he didn't know nothing about me."

"This nigga told him he was fucking your girl and he didn't blast that nigga. I told you them niggas were whores. A nigga couldn't look me in my face and tell me he's fucking my niggas girl, and I don't pull his cap back," Chew said angrily.

"I feel you, but that nigga ain't cut like you and me, that nigga from a whole different tree."

"That's why I say, I don't know why you fuck with them niggas."

"Look here, I'm going to go on and lay my ass down and try to get my mind right for this visit."

"You going to let her know you know?" asked Chew.

"Nah, I'm going to play it for a minute because my shorty is going to be with her, but on my word, when I get out, payback is a bitch."

"I'm here if you need me my nigga," Chew said.

The next morning, Ty-chelle came to visit and she had Corchelle with her. "Hi baby!" she said and tried to kiss Cordell.

Not wanting to expose his hand, he let her kiss him on the lips, but no tongue. "How are you?" he asked.

"Damn! Is that all I get?" she said, rolling her eyes.

For the last couple of months Cordell had seen the change in Ty-chelle, but really didn't pay attention or he just didn't want to believe it. Truth be told, he loved the shit out of Ty-chelle and in a million years he would have never thought she would ever cross him. Boy, how wrong was he.

"You know I don't like doing all that in front of the baby," he said.

"Baby, that girl is a grown woman," she said. "She sees more than that on T.V. and in the hood."

"Probably from her stinking ass mother too," he said under his breath. "She ain't but 6 years old and she don't need to be seeing that," he said.

"Boy, no matter how much you try to shield these kids from the streets, they're still going to see it, cause people don't care no more."

"Ain't that the truth," he said, with an attitude.

"What's wrong with you?" she replied.

"Ty-chelle, you know I love you, but lately somethings have been different between us. If you trust me, I shall never lie to you, but if you lie to me, I shall understand, but never trust you again. I'm going to ask you this one time, have you cheated on me?"

Without even thinking about it, she looked him right in the eyes and said, "Cordell you know I love you and would never do anything to betray your trust."

The line had been drawn right then and there. For the rest of the visit Cordell played with his daughter. Everything that Ty-chelle said went in one ear and out the other because no matter what it was, it was a lie to him cause that's all that could come out of her mouth.

"I will keep my word and pay her back," he thought in his head. "I just don't know how I'm going to do it yet, but I promise, she'll feel just as much pain as I'm feeling now." In the words of his friend, "stinking ass bitch!" And he continued to play with the only woman he'll ever trust again, his daughter.

The day before Chew was to be released, him and Cordell sat under the smoke shack and smoked a black, while they kicked it.

Cordell was happy Chew was going home, but that meant for the next two and a half months, he would be alone or forced to sit and listen to all the "almost" and "getting ready to" ass whoopings Tyson was going to give out.

"Damn my nigga," said Cordell, as he hit the black. "It's me against the world in this motherfucker now."

"Shit, you ain't got but two and a half more months and you'll be out there with us," Chew said as he took the black Cordell was passing him.

Cordell was shaking his head in disappointment, while looking at the ground. "Two and a half months is a long time in this motherfucker, when you ain't got nobody to kick it with."

Chew was feeling the frustration of his friend and wishing he could walk out the door with him.

"Nigga, we ain't nothing but a phone call away. You know me and Moody's going to be together every day, so you'll be able to get through to one of our phones."

"Yeah, I know my nigga, I just wish I were out there with y'all. I know y'all going to be ballin'."

"Trust and believe you're going to have plenty of pictures and the bets are going to be flowing."

"I don't need the bets; my books are straight. I'm just ready to get out of the motherfucker," said Cordell as he took the black from Chew.

"You ain't got that long, plus you can bite off that nigga Tyson," said Chew with a smile on his face, trying to lighten up the mood.

Cordell raised his eyes at Chew with a smirk on his face. "Yeah right."

Laughing, grabbing the black from Cordell and taking a hit, "I feel you my nigga, that nigga is a lame," said Chew.

"What time is Moody going to be here to get you in the morning?" asked Cordell.

"Man, I told that nigga to be here at 8:30, but you know how long it takes those crackers to process a nigga out of here."

"Yeah, they do be taking forever and I think they be taking forever, and I think they be doing that shit on purpose."

"You know they do, that's their way of letting a nigga know they control them until the last second."

"Damn nigga, be like Joe Montana and pass that motherfucking black," said Cordell, looking at Chew playfully. Chew laughed then passed the black which was almost gone. "My fault, a nigga got to thinking about that free world," he said.

"I see. I just hope y'all be careful out there, you know them streets ain't the same," Cordell said.

"Know that's right, but I ain't never been no fool."

"Feel that my nigga. You want me in a game of Madden before the lights go out?" asked Cordell.

"Nigga, you don't want me! But I'll punish you one more time before I leave."

CHAPTER 13

The next morning, Cordell helped Chew to the property room with his stuff. They gave each other a hug and some dap and Chew went on out.

"Well, that's two thirds of B.B.C. on the streets and in a couple of months and some days, we'll all be out there," Cordell thought as he walked to the dorm.

Moody and Chew were sitting at the front of the prison gate waiting on Cordell to get released.

"Finally, all of us are going to be out here to do the damn thing," said Moody.

"That's what I hate about this motherfucker, they quick to book a motherfucker in, but slow to let a motherfucker out," said Chew.

"You know that's right," Moody said, looking around the parking lot at the cars that belong to the people that once told him when to eat, sleep and piss." Man, ain't that Mrs. Davis?"

Chew looked up. "Yeah, that's that stinkin ass bitch! I should cuss that bitch out."

"Nah my nigga," Moody said, laughing. "That bitch might try to press charges on a nigga. You know she hate blacks and she really hate you."

"That bitch put me in the hole three times in less than a year. Stinking ass bitch!"

Cordell was at the property room waiting for the officer to get through inventory for his belongings. "I don't know why they go through this shit. A nigga ain't going to do nothing but throw this shit away," he thought.

"Look man, why don't I donate all this stuff?" he said to the officer.

"I still got to count it," the officer said in reply. "If anything is missing you got to go back and get it, so I hope you didn't give nothing away."

"Man, everything I'm supposed to have is there. I know how y'all play, I been down here too long."

The officer, sensing Cordell had an attitude, took his time. Even stopped a few times to answer the phone. "Nigga want to rush me, I'll show him who's boss," thought the officer.

"This motherfucking cracker is doing this shit on purpose," Cordell said to himself. "I swear, if I ever run into one of these sons of bitches on the streets, I'm going to split their heads to the white meat."

Finally, the officer finished Cordell's inventory and looked at him with a shit-eating grin on his face. "There you go Mr. Jenkins, I hope you enjoyed your stay at our fine institution," he said.

"Another time, another place," said Cordell, as he grabbed his things and walked out the door.

Chew took his focus off Mrs. Davis as Cordell was coming out the gate. "About time they let my nigga out."

"What took you ass so long? We been out here for 40 minutes! We were almost in there to get your ass. This crazy motherfucker here wanted to cuss out Mrs. Davis, knowing how nasty the hoe is," said Moody.

"Fuck that stinking ass bitch!" Chew said.

"That dick sucking officer wanted to take his time with a niggas shit," Cordell said as he admired Moody's car. It was a brand-new Cadillac, triple white, sitting on 24's and it had beat. "Damn, this is a pretty motherfucker here," he said.

"Nigga wait until you see Chew's shit," Moody said.

"Damn nigga, why you want to put business out there like that?" said Chew, grinning from ear to ear cause he knew his whip was one of the coldest in the city.

They rode and talked about all the shit they have been through in the joint and what was happening in the streets. Moody told Cordell about his connect, the prices he was getting and how fast the shit was moving. Chew put him up on who was doing what and who was in the way. They talked about what needed to be done and how they were going to do it.

B.B.C. was in full effect and they all vowed that "money over bitches" and "death before dishonor" will be the code they would live by. They raised their cups and toasted to "Ball til we fall!"

Moody dropped Cordell off at his mother's house where her and his daughter were waiting. As soon as he got out the car, his daughter ran out the door and jumped in his arms, "Daddy!"

"How is daddy's precious angel doing?" he said as he hugged her tight and shut the car door.

"Holla at us later, " Moody said as they pulled away and let Cordell enjoy his time with his family.

Although his mother came to see him twice a month, it seemed like forever since he last saw her. He walked up to the porch still with his daughter in his arms and gave his mother a kiss on the cheek.

"How are you doing son?"

"I'm alright, just glad to be home."

"What are you going to do to stay home?"

"I'm going to do everything possible, but I ain't going to starve out here."

"Son, you know I love you and I always will, but all I ask is that you stay out of trouble, that child needs you."

"Yeah!" Corchelle added, hugging him tighter.

"Look ma, you gave me everything I ever needed and wanted, and I love you for that, but I got to do the same for mine. You know I have never lied to you and I never will. Ever since I walked off that field, which was the biggest mistake of my life, I didn't know nothing but the streets. I'm going to get a job because I know that's what you want me to do. I will do anything to make you happy, but I'm going to hustle too."

"I will never condone your lifestyle, but you are my child and I will always be there for you whenever you need me, but all I ask is that you be careful out there."

"I will," he said as they all walked in the house together. "You didn't tell Ty-chelle I was coming home today, did you?"

"No, you told me not to. I just told her I was coming to get Corchelle for a little while."

"That's cool. Thanks mom!"

Cordell's mom pulled up in front of Ty-chelle's house and blew the horn and within a few minutes she came to the door. She watched as her baby girl made her way up the steps. She gave her a hug and waved bye to her daughter's grandmother.

"Are you hungry?" she asked.

"No, I ate at my granny's house."

"What else did you do at your granny's? Did you have a good time?" Ty-chelle asked trying to pick her daughter for information.

"I saw my daddy," she said happily.

Ty-chelle thought for a minute, knowing that her daughter was not gone long enough to make the trip to see her father.

"You didn't see your daddy; did he call over your granny's?"

"My daddy was at my granny's house."

"Oh, you saw a picture of your daddy at your granny's house?"

"No, mommy! My daddy was over my granny's house. His friends dropped him off this morning. I got to hug him, and we talked, then me, him and my granny went out shopping for his clothes."

Ty-chelle thought with confusion, "I know this motherfucker didn't get out and not bring his ass here! What kind of game is this nigga trying to play?" She picked up the phone and started dialing his mother's house.

"Hello," Cordell said.

"What's up?" Ty-chelle replied.

"What you mean what's up?"

"So, you just going to get out of prison and not tell me?" she asked.

"Damn, you funny," he said. "Since when did we have to tell each other everything?"

"I know you ain't on no bullshit Cordell, the way I had my ass on that highway faithfully for 6 motherfucking years?"

"Just because you come visit me, I'm obligated to be with you?"

"What's wrong with you? Before you left, we was together, during the whole time you've been locked up we've been together and now that you're home it's something different?"

"Babe look, I ain't going to play no games with you, I'm always going to be there for my shorty, but me and you ain't got no rap unless it's about her."

"Why Cordell, what did I do wrong?" she asked crying in the phone.

Usually her tears would have gotten to him and he would have folded, but today, he didn't care how much she cried. She violated his trust and that is something he could never forgive.

"I told you if ever you lie to me I shall understand, but never trust you again. I can't be with a woman I can't trust."

"You can trust me Cordell, I will never lie to you, I promise!"

This made him even more angry. "You'll never lie to me, you promise?! Well, who the fuck is Aaron?"

Ty-chelle was stunned. Those few nights when she got lonely and needed to be touched, Aaron was there for her. She never thought anyone would ever know and now stood to lose the only man she ever loved; her child's father. To make matters worse, the sex wasn't even that good.

"Yeah, that's what I thought, you can't say shit, can you?" he said.

"Cordell, you just don't understand, six years was a long time and it was only three times."

"Three times! One is one too many and then the nigga told Doe you didn't even tell him about me."

"So, Doe told you? Did he tell you that Leo tried to holla at me? Nah, I bet he didn't tell you that, did he?"

Now Cordell was the one confused and didn't know what to think or say. "Well, he should've fucked you too!" and slammed the phone down on the receiver.

For the next few hours, Ty-chelle tried to talk to Cordell. Every time she reached him by blocking out the number or having one of her friends call on three way, he would hang up on her. It was over and she was starting to realize that cause one thing he doesn't do is forget, let alone, forgive.

Cordell didn't know what to think. Would Leo try him like that and try to fuck his baby's mother? "I know Leo would fuck anything and would do anything for some pussy, but I can't see him trying to fuck Ty-chelle, knowing I would fuck him up," he said to himself.

Maybe she was just trying to get me mad because she knows she's busted, and I'm done with her ass, he thought.

CHAPTER 14

Cordell called Doe and told him to come and pick him up. An hour later, they were sitting in the car together.

"Let me ask you something. Ty-chelle told me that Leo tried to come on to her. Did you know about that?"

"Nah, man I didn't know nothing about that. Do you believe her?"

"I don't know. You know how Leo is, always trying to fuck something."

"Yeah, but I don't see him trying her," said Doe. "We all know the rules, ain't no fun unless the homies can have some, but main girls and baby mamas are off limits."

"Sometimes niggas forget the rules and I pray that nigga didn't forget about that one," Cordell said meaning every word.

"If he did some shit like that, it's fucked up and he needs to be checked."

"Call that nigga and find out where he at so I can talk to him face to face."

Leo was at the car wash. Cordell and Doe pulled in right behind his car. Cordell was the first out of the car.

"What's good my nigga?" said Cordell looking at Leo hard.

"Shit, nothing," Leo said while still drying off his car.

"Look here man, we go too far back to be bullshitting each other. So, I'm just going to come out and ask you. You try to hit on my baby mama?"

"Who, Ty-chelle?" he said with a look of surprise.

Cordell could tell by the way he said her name and the look in his eyes that it was probably true. He didn't want to jump to conclusions, and he hoped his onetime best friend would be honest with him.

"Who else, she the only baby mama I got that I know of anyway."

"She tells you some shit like that?"

Cordell was really starting to get angry because Leo was beating around the bush. He wouldn't even keep an eye contact with him anymore.

"Look, my nigga, fuck who told me, all I need to know is if it's true or not," Cordell asked impatiently. "If you did, it's fucked up, but I understand. After all, she wasn't being faithful anyway."

"I can't believe she told you some shit like that, especially the way we're looking out," Leo said.

"Fuck how y'all was looking out, cause we know the rules. Baby mamas, main girls and anybody we know the other has feelings for, are off limits. So, I'm gonna ask you one more fucking time, is it true?"

"So, man, after everything you and I have been through, you going to come at me about some bitch who was cheating on you anyway?"

Cordell couldn't hold it in any longer and popped the shit out of Leo. Leo fell to the ground trying to get up. But everytime he tried, he fell back down. Cordell grabbed his pistol from his waist and put it to Leo's head. "Nigga if you ever disrespect me like that again, I will kill you!" Then he slapped him with the butt of the gun.

"Cordell!" Doe called. "Come on man, we boys, we better than that."

"Fuck that nigga!" Cordell shouted, spitting at Leo's while he laid on the ground. "That nigga ain't no boy, friend or nothing of mine," he said then kicked him in the face.

Doe grabbed Cordell and told him to get in the car. People started gathering around and sooner or later the police would be there.

When they were about three blocks away, Doe's phone rang. "Hello."

"Nigga! that was fucked up and tell that nigga I got him, he shouldn't have never put his hands on me," Leo shouted.

"You know you was wrong," said Doe.

"How was I wrong, I don't remember that shit, if I did it, it was one of them nights I was fucked up and didn't know what I was doing."

"Why didn't you just tell the nigga that in the first place?"

"That nigga didn't give me a chance, but that's alright, I'm going to get the last laugh," Leo said and hung up in Doe's ear.

Doe looked over at Cordell, "Man, you are fucked up."

"Nah, he is fucked up! You know I would never try to hollar at Leo's baby mama."

"I know, but you didn't have to do him like that in front of all them people. I think that hurt him the most."

Cordell didn't respond. He just sat there staring out the window, knowing deep inside that he was wrong. Leo was his dog and he overreacted. He also knew that one day, he knows he's going to have to pay for it.

He wasn't worried about Leo coming after him cause he wasn't no killer or fighter, but he knew too much. For a moment, Cordell thought about killing him, but he couldn't see himself doing that. He still had too much love for him, even after he disrespected him. "Drop me off at the house," he finally said.

CHAPTER 15

Cordell took a shower and put on some clothes, then called Chew and told him about what happened with Leo. Chew laughed and told him he should have killed him. "I feel bad about that shit," Cordell said. "It's supposed to be money over bitches, and I flipped."

"Shit, ain't no need in feeling bad, even though it's money over bitches, you never considered your baby mama a bitch, even when she done you wrong. To me, all them whores are bitches."

Cordell laughed, "Why you so hard on women? Somebody done broke your heart and you want to take it out on all women."

"Nah playboy, ain't nobody broke the Chew's heart and I'll never let one of them stinkin ass bitches get that close."

"What about that one chick you used to cry to me and Moody about when we were on the yard?"

"Go on with that bullshit nigga."

"So, what's up tonight?"

"Let me call Moody and see what he wants to do, we'd probably go to 537."

"Shit, the last time I was at that motherfucker, it cost me 10 years," said Cordell.

"It's an older crowd now, all them young and wild motherfuckers like you used to be, who shoot up everything, they go to the Velvet now."

"Like I used to be? Man, we ain't going to get on the conversation again, like we did in the joint, are we?" Cordell said.

"What are you talking about? So, you're trying to say you wasn't one of those wild motherfuckers who shot up the club 7 years ago?"

"Nah, I'm not saying that at all, but you got your nerve talking about a motherfucker wanting to shoot up some shit.

If I'm Jesse James, you got to be Billy the kid and that damn Moody is Doc Holiday."

"Nigga, you are silly," Chew said, laughing. "Plus, them one cats that used to own Billy's, own it now and they don't play that wild shit."

"Cool then, I'm already dressed for success, so come get me and hit Moody up on the way."

"Got you my nigga. I'm on my way."

An hour later, Chew pulled up in his big boy Lexus. That motherfucker is right, Cordell thought to himself as he came out the door. It was the biggest Lexus he'd ever seen, candy apple red and it looked like the motherfucker was dipped in a hundred coats of candy paint. The guts were white, trimmed in red with red letters across each seat, B.B.C.

TV's were everywhere, one in the steering wheel for the driver, one built in the glove box cover for the passenger and in the back of both headrests for the people in the back. Music so loud it shook every house on the block. Plus, to top it off, it was sitting on 26's.

Chew turned down the music when Cordell got inside of the car, smiling at the look on Cordell's face. "So, what do you think?"

"I see what Moody was talking about, this is a bad motherfucker. Plus, I see you representing with our logo on the seats," said Cordell.

"B.B.C. baby! Black Billionaires Club, ball til we fall, ain't that what we said in the joint?"

"Got that right my nigga and any motherfucker who gets in our way and tries to shatter this dream can get it," Cordell said, thinking about that lame Leo. "So, what Moody saying?" he said, coming out of his thoughts.

"He said he's going to meet us at the club and save us a parking space."

"I really hope these niggas don't be tripping like they used to. I ain't been out the joint a week yet and I ain't trying to go back," Cordell said.

"Trust me my nigga, it ain't like that no more. Plus, fuck it if a nigga gets it wrong, you ain't got to do shit, cause I'm going to bunk head bounce them."

"Nigga you know I ain't above getting my hands dirty."

"I was getting ready to say, these motherfucking crackers done scared you straight?"

"Never that!" said Cordell, seriously.

They pulled into the parking lot and Moody was waiting on them. They parked next to him and played the parking lot, hollering at every bitch that was worth hollering at, and of course, Chew called every one of them stinking ass bitches to their faces.

That is how pretty much the next six months went. Though they were not billionaires yet, they had plenty of money and they trusted and believed that they were going to get there, if it was up to them.

Cordell looked out for Doe and Doe looked out for Leo. Even though Doe was taking his dope sharing with Leo, Cordell didn't even trip about it. To be honest, he was kinda glad Leo was getting a little money, after all, they used to be best friends.

He even got a job to satisfy his mother at this company as a security guard. Every time he thought about that, it made him laugh. Moody and Chew used to give him the blues, especially Chew.

"A nigga who done murdered, shot up niggas and sells more dope than a Walgreens pharmacy, a motherfucking security guard," he would often say.

He wasn't allowed to carry a gun because he was a convicted felon, but you know the saying, better to get caught with it than without it," he always said when Moody joked with him about it. He was always on time, no matter how late he stayed out the night before.

This was his first job, and to him, it was the best thing to happen to him. Not only did he make his mother happy and account for some of his toys, he met her, the fallen angel, his soul mate and the only woman besides his mother and daughter, who would love him unconditionally.

CHAPTER 16

Gina was 5'3", caramel brown complexion without a blemish on her beautiful face. Her hair was black and hung down past her shoulders. She had perfect full lips that had Cordell licking his own in anticipation of one day feeling them against his. Her eyes were hazel brown and when the light hit them right, a touch of gold could be seen around the pupils.

He might have been imagining the last part, but it was no doubt he was hooked from the very first time he looked into them.

He didn't believe in love at first sight, especially since he promised himself that he would never trust another woman. He never broke his word, but he couldn't explain what he was feeling.

It was his first day on the job and he was making his rounds, as he was shown how to do by his boss. When he got to her department, he was able to see her even better and what he saw from a distance was amazing and he didn't think it could get any better. It did. What he saw was unbelievable. She was the most beautiful woman he had ever seen in his life.

She wasn't supermodel beautiful, which he thought those types were fake anyway. They needed make up and all kinds of other stuff to perfect their beauty. Her beauty was natural, like an angel who had fallen from the sky.

She turned and looked at him and from that moment on he was stuck. "Can I help you?" she asked, and he couldn't speak or at least the words didn't come out. "Excuse me, are you okay?" she then said, which broke him out of his trance.

"Yeah, I'm okay," he said. "I was just thinking about something and went off in a daze." This fucked Cordell up because he was smooth when it came to the ladies and this woman had him mesmerized.

"It looked like you were sleep walking with your eyes open," she said.

"I've been known to do that sometimes. By the way, my name is Cordell and I'm the new security guard."

She looked him up and down with those beautiful eyes and then turned around and went back to working on her computer.

This never happened to Cordell before and it make him want her even more. "Oh, so you want to play hard to get?" he thought to himself. "She must not know who I am, but she will!" Then he walked away.

Gina was working on her computer when she felt someone staring at her, so she turned around. She saw Cordell standing there looking at her. "Damn, who is this handsome ass man staring at me? It must be the new security guard every woman in here been talking about," she thought to herself.

When Cordell finally spoke, he told her his name and she looked him over with a keen eye and admiration. "I guess I'm just supposed to drop my panties cause he's fine and he told me his name. That's what he's probably used to, but he got the wrong one here, right now anyway," she thought and then turned around and finished her work.

As he was leaving, she had to get one more look. "Damn, that nigga looks familiar, but I can't picture where I know him from. It doesn't matter, I'll have him anyway," she said to herself.

For the next three weeks, they played a game of cat and mouse. One day Cordell would be the cat, chasing Gina and the next day Gina would be the cat, chasing Cordell.

Finally, Gina gave Cordell her number. "Don't put my number on the wall in the bathroom," she said.

"Baby, as hard as I've worked for this piece of paper here, it ain't going on no wall or in no black book," he said.

"Oh, so you do got a little black book that you collect numbers in?"

"Nah beautiful, it ain't like that. Now I done had my share of women, I ain't going to lie about that, but none that can compare to you."

"How many times you done used that line?"

"Trust and believe, I don't have to use lines, you are probably the first woman I've ever had to chase."

"So, women just throw themselves at you. Who do you think you are?" she said, knowing that it was probably true cause he was one fine motherfucker.

"You really don't know who I am do you?" he said, making him realize how special she really is because she doesn't want his name or his money.

"Am I supposed to? Are you famous or something?" she said, rolling her head.

"Girl you are something else, but that's what I like about you. I'll make sure this number doesn't find the bathroom wall," he said as he was walking off.

"Yeah, you do that," she said, really trying to figure out who he was. "I'm going to have to call LaShonda, she knows everybody," she thought.

She picked up the phone and dialed LaShonda's work number. "Hello, LaShonda Wilson speaking, may I help you?" the voice on the other end of the phone said.

"Girl, are you busy?" she said.

"Nah, not forreal, what's up?"

"You ever heard of a nigga name Cordell Jenkins cause this nigga act like he's famous or something?"

"Bitch, who don't know Cordell?" LaShonda said.

"Shit, I don't."

"Gina come on, where you been? Remember about seven years ago we were at 537 and that nigga Dino and Snaps shot up the parking lot and then they ended up getting killed?"

"Yeah, I remember that."

"Well, he's the nigga that killed them. He used to be a football star, but now he runs with these other two niggas who's getting paper and they call themselves B.B.C., Black Billionaires Club."

"I heard about them, but this nigga don't look like no billionaire to me, working up in this motherfucker."

"He works there?" LaShonda asked confused. "Girl, don't let that nigga fool you, they might not be billionaires yet, but they are on their way."

"Plus LaShonda, ain't that the nigga you were trying to push all up on that night that shit popped off?" Gina asked.

"Yeah, that's him, but he wasn't looking at me. It takes a special kind of female to get him. His baby mama done something and now he don't trust no female. Why you are asking so many questions about him?"

"He's been trying to get at me, but if you were trying to get at him, I'm cool. I ain't going to fuck with him."

"Nah Gina, it wasn't like that and if that nigga is trying to get at you, you would be a fool to let him get away."

"I'll call you when I get home tonight," Gina said and hung up the phone, intrigued by what she just heard.

For the rest of the day, it was hard for her to concentrate on her work because all she could think about was Cordell.

CHAPTER 17

Cordell decided to take care of a little business before he hooked up with Moody and Chew. He went to his spot to see what he was working with.

His spot was a secluded area of the city. Still he circled the block a few times to make sure he wasn't followed. The jackers knew he was a killer and took no shorts, but even a nigga with sense could get hungry enough to try King Kong for his bananas.

Once he knew that he wasn't followed, he pulled in the back of the stash house, looked in the rear-view mirror and pulled out his pistol just in case he missed something.

He checked his supply and was ready to start making calls. His first call was to his cousin cause he usually runs through his shit. That takes care of half the stash.

He then called all his runners to make sure they were straight and even some of the other big dope boys he was supplying.

One thing he hated was to be out kicking it and a motherfucker calls for some work and he had to stop what he was doing to handle business cause they were going to live up to their name B.B.C., and it was going to take every dime they could get.

Doe was one of the main ones who called him right when he was getting ready to get in some pussy or walking into the door of the club, needing some work. "Let me call this nigga," he said.

"Who this?" Doe said.

"Nigga you know who this is. I know you got my number programmed in your phone. I just hope you ain't got my name in that motherfucker."

"Nah playboy, I ain't got your name, I got C-murder next to it."

"If that motherfucker gets into the wrong hands, I hope they don't put two and two together cause I'll C- you to murder you," said Cordell.

"You ain't got to worry about that, I'll eat any charge come my way and die in prison before I sign statements on a nigga."

"Feel that. I was just calling you to make sure you're straight on the work tip before I head out later on. You know how you are, always waiting to the last minute when a nigga enjoying himself."

"I should be straight until tomorrow anyway," said Doe. "What y'all doing tonight?"

"I don't know. I got to call Moody and Chew back to see what's up."

"I'll probably hook up with Leo and see what we can get into."

"How's he doing anyway?" Cordell asked, kind of missing his old partner. It had been almost a year since they kicked it. "He still don't fuck with me?"

"He's cool. He said he wasn't even tripping about that shit anymore."

"Guess he ain't. Shit, he's eating off of me. Does he know that work you giving him is coming from me?"

"He knows and trust me, he's grateful."

"Well hit me up tomorrow and don't wait to the last minute."

"Alright my nigga, peace," Doe said, then hung up.

"Well, that's out of the way," said Cordell. I wonder what Gina is doing?" He looked in his hiding spot and pulled out the piece of paper.

"I don't know why I'm still hiding numbers and shit; I don't have no girlfriend." He found the paper he was looking for and dialed the number. After about four rings, a female answered the phone. "Hello," she said.

"Is Gina there?" asked Cordell in a soft bedroom voice.

"Who is this?" the female asked.

Curious as to who would be asking all these questions, for what he understood about Gina, is that she lived by herself and wasn't the type to have people all up in her business. "Cordell!" he finally responded.

There was a loud scream, which made Cordell pull the phone away from his ear and then he heard a familiar voice. A voice that sounded like it came from heaven. "Hello," Gina said.

"Damn baby, what was all that?" asked Cordell.

"My stupid ass friend acting like she don't have no damn sense," she said, staring at her friend LaShonda like she was crazy. LaShonda was looking back at her with a silly smile on her face, watching every move Gina made and trying to hear her conversation. So, Gina went into the bedroom and shut the door.

"What are you doing right now?" he asked.

"Getting ready to go out," she replied.

"Well look, I know you said you lived off 7th and Broadway, I'm almost at the White Castle, think I can stop by and see you before you roll out?"

Thinking about it for a minute because she was feeling the shit out of Cordell, but she knew how silly LaShonda can get and she didn't want him to judge her by her friends. Plus, she knew LaShonda tried to get at him, and everybody knew she was a freak. "What would he think about me if he knew I hung around her?" she thought to herself.

"Fuck it!" she said to herself. "Sure, you can stop by. I'm two blocks up, third house from the corner you'll see my car."

Excited and pleased that she invited him over, but realizing she's not alone, and knowing how girls could get when other girls are around. For some reason, he didn't think she was like that, but tried to be courteous. "I see you're not alone; your friends won't mind me intruding, will they?"

"First of all, this is my house and I say who comes and goes. Secondly, I don't live for my friends, I live for Gina!" she said aggressively.

Pleased at her response, which confirmed what he felt about her, as being a strong, independent, beautiful, black woman, he said, "Okay, lil mama! No harm intended."

A few minutes later, he pulled up to her house and got out of the car. She came out to meet him. He looked behind her and saw her two friends standing in the door. He recognized one of them, he thought, but she was too far away to be for sure.

"Damn shorty, you got bodyguards?" he said as he nodded his head towards the door.

She turned and looked back at her friends standing in the doorway giggling. "Don't pay them no attention," she said, pulling him away from the side of the car to the back.

"So, where you are going tonight?" he asked, not trying to sound possessive, but curious, hoping she was going to say 537 because tonight was when he was going to break his truck out.

"We're going to 537 and then probably to the Waffle House afterwards."

"Who's driving?"

"Not me," she said. "I'm trying to get my drink on."

"That's cool, how about this?" he said grabbing her hand and when she didn't pull it away, he started rubbing it between his, "why don't you ride to the Waffle House with me and I'll bring you home."

"I'll let you know later," she said, looking at him suspiciously.

Catching on to the look she was giving him, he said, "Shorty, it ain't even like that, all I want to do is spend some time with you, that's all."

"Well, if that's all, then I guess we can do that. I'll let my girls know."

"I'll holla at you at the club then," he said and then kissed her on the cheek.

Blushing from ear to ear, she slowly let go of his hand, "You do that."

Her friends were still in the door when she went in. Cordell heard them screaming and knew it was because of him. He started the car and turned up the music. Jay Z's "Me and my girlfriend" started blasting out of the speaker as he pulled off.

CHAPTER 18

Cordell pulled up in his flip flop white Escalade he just got out of the shop that morning. It had plush leather seats, black trimmed in white and just like Chew and Moody, had "B.B.C." on the seats.

It had six T.V.'s, a PlayStation 2 and an Xbox. It was sitting on 28" rims, with music so clear you thought Nelly was in concert. To top it off, every piece of metal was dipped in chrome.

Everyone in the crowd was looking with deep admiration and a few with envy. He parked beside Chew's Lexus and got out. This was the first time Chew or Moody saw the truck since he put it in the shop.

"Nigga, you always got to put on a show, don't you?" Chew said, looking inside the truck with a smile on his face.

Moody joined him, "Shit, if you got it, why not floss it."

"You know that's right," said Cordell, lifting up the back door, grabbing one of the joy sticks to the Xbox. Chew came and grabbed the other one.

The crowd got bigger as him and Chew played Madden and talked shit to each other, like they did on the yard. Moody was entertaining a group of females behind them as they played.

"What does B.B.C. stand for?" one of the girls asked Moody.

"Black Billionaires Club, baby," said Moody with a smile on his face.

Looking at him wide eyed and with dollar signs in her eyes, "So y'all billionaires?" she stated more than asked.

"Nah, not yet, but as long as we can dream it, we can obtain it and this is a reminder of our goal," Moody responded.

Already knowing who they were, she was trying to play dumb, hoping a nigga wouldn't think she was on the come up like every other sack chaser in the city. "So, what are y'all into?" she asked with a curious look on her face.

Chew, getting tired of all the questions, put the joystick down and turned around, looked dead in her eyes, and said, "Bitch, you the police or something, asking all these damn questions?"

Moody, Cordell and everybody in the crowd fell out laughing. She stood there with her mouth wide open. "Excuse me!" she said and then walked away with her friends, rolling her eyes at Chew. He didn't even give a fuck.

"Nigga, you are fucked up," Cordell said to Chew, still laughing trying to catch his breath.

Chew had to crack a smile himself. "I hate when them stinking ass bitches ask a hundred damn questions about shit that ain't their business. And this nigga here," he said pointing at Moody, "act like he's giving an interview and shit."

The crowd started to move away from them and divided up into smaller individual groups, like they were before he pulled in. It was still a few females around, but they watched what they asked, they didn't want to be the next one to get clowned.

Cordell heard someone clear their throat behind him. He turned around, it was Gina. "How you doing, lil mama?" he asked, surprised to see her. "I thought you would be in the club by now."

Looking at the girls standing around looking at her, she raised her brow and pulled him off to the side. "I seen you over here, so I decided to make my presence felt," she said, batting her beautiful eyes.

"Baby girl, you can make you presence felt anytime I'm around," he said, grabbing her hand.

"Whose truck is this?" she asked as she stepped back to get a better look.

"Who else?" he answered as he led her to the driver's side of the door, opened it and got in. He sat with his legs out and pulled her between his legs. She didn't resist, and for the first time, he felt how natural being with her felt.

They stood there talking about their plans for tonight. Cordell saw Ty-chelle walking up toward them. This was the first time he saw her since that shit with Leo. He had been having his mother go pick up Corchelle and bring her to him.

Ty-chelle stood in front of them rolling her eyes at Gina with her fists on her hips. "Cordell can I talk to you for a minute?" she said, while still looking at Gina.

"Look Ty-chelle, me and you ain't got no rap for each other. You did you and I respect that, but now I'm doing me and I'm happy where I'm at," he said, pulling Gina even closer, not to make Ty-chelle jealous, but to show Gina that he's feeling her forreal.

Gina's friend LaShonda came around to the side of the truck and asked Gina if she was alright, looking at Ty-chelle a "bitch if you want your issue, you can get it right here" look.

Gina sensing her friend's eagerness to get in Ty-chelle's ass, said, "I'm alright," then kissed Cordell on his cheek. "I'm going to let you and your baby mama talk. We still on for breakfast, right?"

"No question!" he said as he watched Gina walk off and remembered LaShonda. That's why that girl looked familiar when I saw her standing in the door, he thought.

Turning his focus back to Ty-chelle, "Look, I don't know what's going through your head, but you know where we stand."

She moved closer to Cordell and he held his hand out to stop her. She looked at him in his face, as the tears started coming down her face.

He tried to fight back his emotions, but he couldn't lie to himself, seeing the mother of his child crying crushed him. He remembered when he talked to her on the phone when he first came home and her tears didn't faze him, but now, she was right here in his face.

"Cordell, I know you're mad at me. I done some dumb shit. I was lonely and my lust got the best of me. I wasn't trying to replace you, hell, nobody can do that," she said, looking hard into his eyes, as he turned away from her glance. She grabbed his hand and pulled it to her chest, "Cordell, I'm sorry. Please give us another chance. I promise I won't let you down again."

Feeling that he was about to explode at her promise, remembering on that visit how she promised she had been faithful to him when the whole time she had fucked another nigga, he pulled his hands away from her chest and got down out of his truck. "Ty-chelle, in order to open new doors we must close old ones, and I thought I done that when we discussed this when I came home. Evidently, it wasn't clear. You betrayed me and even if I wanted to forgive you, I couldn't forget. I will always love you cause you're my daughter's mother, but I would never respect you for what you done. I can never be with a woman that I don't respect."

"Do you respect that girl who was standing between your legs?" she asked.

"Very much," he said as he kissed her on the cheek and went towards the club, leaving her standing there with tears in her eyes, watching him walk away.

Peter Gunnz and his righthand man, Fast Black, were sitting in the car behind the dark tint watching the crowd as they were going and coming in and out of club 537. Their purpose was to catch somebody slipping, and they seldom failed at this task.

From where they sat, they could see everybody, but hardly anybody could see them. They counted on this because every stick-up crew out there knew the element of surprise was their best weapon.

There were a lot of stick up crews out there, but none were as bold, ruthless and hungry as the one ran by Peter Gunnz. His team was on everybody's watch for list, the drug dealers, hustlers and even the police.

Besides Peter Gunnz and Black, there was Murder. He was the baby of the crew, only sixteen years old. It had been said that he was responsible for three unsolved murders, but everybody knew it was a lot more.

Then there was Sincere, he was the quiet one and very sneaky. Always on point. Rarely did he ever pull a pistol and not use it. Gunnz primarily used him as the driver. His philosophy was shoot first, ask questions later. This caused a lot of problems sometimes. They would have to leave before they had all the money or dope cause he had shot somebody.

Then Soldier Slim, he had a smooth baby face. He could get next to a lot of people that the rest of them couldn't. He was ruthless with a Capital "R" and probably the coldest of the crew next to Gunnz, but he was the smartest.

For years, robbery and homicide detectives have been trying to put cases on them, which is the mythology behind the name of their crew. Not only were they wanted by the police, but also by the few niggas they robbed of major bread and spared their lives.

It was rumored that Gunnz and Black had over a hundred grand on their heads and the other three had fifty grand on theirs. Though the money sounded good to anyone who wanted to collect the bounty, the repercussions of failure just wasn't worth the reward. This enhanced the name "Louisville's Most Wanted" or "LMW" as they like to call themselves.

Gunnz was looking around when he noticed the flip flop white Escalade pull into the parking lot at the back of the club. He watched as it pulled up next to the candy apple red Lexus and the triple black Caddy. He knew the Lexus belonged to Chew and the Caddy to Moody, who were members of B.B.C., then he saw Cordell exit the driver seat and come to the back.

He knew it would be dangerous to try and jack them niggas, cause they had a reputation for putting a niggas dick in the dirt. However, sometimes that was the price you pay to play the game the way they played it and somewhere down the line he was going to try them niggas.

He tapped Black on his leg to get his attention. "Look over there," he pointed towards Cordell and his crew, "that motherfucking truck Cordell got is right."

Black, sitting all the way up in his seat to get a better look, "Damn!" he said, admiring the paint job, TV's, rims and sound system.

"He must've just got that cause I ain't seen him in it before tonight," said Gunnz.

"I heard he was supposed to break something nice out soon, but I didn't expect it to be nothing like that there. I knew them niggas were getting paper, but all them niggas are riding pretty. That's some shit you break out for Derby, not the summer," Black said, while looking back and forth between the Escalade, Lexus and Caddy.

Curious with his eyes still glued on the three B.B.C. members with dollar signs in his eyes, Gunnz asked Black, "How did you hear about him breaking something out soon? Do they have a loose mouth in the circle?"

"Cordell got a cousin named Tony, who does a lot of fronting for the females, and in the process, he put a lot of their business out there."

A thought came to Gunnz' head and usually when something comes to his mind he follows through with it. "Interesting," he said, smiling to himself.

Black, looked at his partner, reading his mind. He wasn't no bitch, but he knew his partner was thinking about trying these niggas. If they didn't come correct it would be their last lick and that was for sure. "Yeah, them niggas got their shit together forreal!" hoping his partner would take the hint.

Gunnz, sensing his partners apprehension said, "If I ever catch one of them niggas slipping, their asses are mine!"

Relieved that Gunnz wasn't thinking about doing something stupid like trying these niggas tonight, Black said, "Let's find one of these other suckers to relieve of their possessions," as he looked around the lot while watching Cordell enter the club.

Cordell entered the club and found Gina sitting at a table with her friends. He walked over to her, she smiled at him as he pulled up a chair and sat down next to her. He went in his pocket, pulled out a bill and told her friends to go get them a drink. He should have known that LaShonda would be the first one to reach for the money.

Gina looked at him and she could tell he was a little upset about the way his baby's mama had approached them outside. "Are you okay?" she asked and grabbed his hand. He lifted his head and gave a genuine smile. "I am not," he said and kissed her for the first time.

They talked and laughed together for the rest of the night. When the crowd started thinning out, they left the club and went to breakfast at the Waffle House.

He pulled up at her house to drop her off and kissed her one more time. This time it was very passionate. She fought against her better judgment and asked him if he wanted to come in. "I'm going to let you know right now, we ain't going to do nothing," she said, even though she really wanted to, but she wasn't the type to have sex on the first date.

"Of course, I do, and I want you to know we ain't doing nothing," he said as he locked the doors and turned on the alarm with the keyless remote.

She opened the door and they went to the basement, where the bar was and had another drink. This time, more pop than liquor. After all, it was 5:30 in the morning. They finished their drink and she led him upstairs to her bedroom. He looked around to make sure she didn't have any mens clothes laying around. "I sleep naked," he said. " I hope that don't bother you."

She looked at him suspiciously. "Do you?" was all she said and took her clothes off and put on a long tee shirt.

They held each other and got used to the way each of them felt, being touched by the other. "So, this is what intimacy feels like, huh?" Cordell asked, kissing her softly.

"Do you like it?" she asked in response.

"I like it very much, in fact, I never want it to end."

For the next six months, they worked together, played together and was pretty much inseparable. They bought a house together and started building a wonderful life as one.

Gina and Ty-chelle had a few problems with each other. Ty-chelle wouldn't allow Corchelle to come and stay at their house, but Cordell put that in check really quick. Ty-chelle knew not to fuck with him.

CHAPTER 19

Doe and Leo were driving down Broadway when Officer Thompson spotted Doe's car. "You see who that is?" he said to his partner, Officer Weaver.

Thompson and Weaver were two of the dirtiest drug officers or Narc's in Louisville and they had a hard-on for Cordell and his B.B.C. crew. "That's Doe, ain't it?" Weaver asked.

"Yeah, that's that fat motherfucker. I wonder if he got some dope on him?" said Thompson.

"I doubt it, but if we can ever catch them wrong, I'm sure they'll give up Cordell to save their own asses. Especially Leo, he's the weakest link," Weaver said.

"Fuck it, let's pull them over anyway. Never know, they might have dropped some on accident."

"I hope they try to run; I wouldn't mind shooting Doe in that fat ass of his," smiled Weaver.

Doe spotted the Narcs in the rear-view mirror. "Damn, here comes them dick suckers Thompson and Weaver," he said to Leo.

"Nigga, you ain't dirty, are you?" Leo asked him while glancing at him briefly.

"Nah, but I got the pistol under the seat."

"It's clean, ain't it?"

"I hope so, I brought it from that fiend Marcus," Doe said.

"Ain't no telling where Marcus stole it from, but I doubt it got a body on it. Niggas ain't going to leave no hot pistol around for him to steal."

"Damn, they just hit the lights." Doe pulled over to the curb and turned the car off.

Officer Thompson pulled over behind them. "Doe, put your hands where I can see them. You do the same Leo," he said, calling them by their street names, as if they were buddies, knowing dealers hate that.

They walked up to Doe's car, not even putting their hands on their guns because they knew Doe and Leo were just flunkies. If it had been Cordell, their guns would have been out when they first spotted the car.

"How you are doing fellas?" Weaver said.

"Man, why y'all fucking with us when we ain't did shit?" said Doe.

"Got any drugs on you?" asked Thompson.

"Drugs? We don't sell drugs," said Leo.

"Listen to this guy, he should be doing stand-up on somebody's stage," Weaver laughed.

"Then again, they might not. You know Doe here was once the man, now he got to wait on Cordell to spoon feed him," Thompson said, trying to push a button in Doe.

"Y'all don't know what the fuck y'all talking about. I don't sell drugs period and if I did, I wouldn't sell them for nobody else," said Doe.

"Yeah, alright. Step out of the car," Thompson said.

"For what?" said Doe.

"Cause we asked you to," Weaver added.

"Why y'all pull us over in the first place?" asked Leo.

"Who the police, you or us? We ask the motherfucking question," Thompson said.

"Now get your asses out of the motherfucking car!" Weaver stated.

Knowing they didn't have a win in this situation, Doe and Leo got out of the car and put their hands on the hood. "Now that's better," said Thompson, as they handcuffed them.

They searched the car and when Weaver ran his hand under the passenger seat, he felt the gun. Grabbing it with the tip of his fingers, he held it up. "Look what we got here. Now which one of y'all going to claim this?"

Doe and Leo both said, "It ain't mine," as if they were twins connected at the hip.

"Well, since neither of you wants to claim it, it's both of yours," said Thompson.

"Works for me," Weaver said. "You find anything else?"

"Nah, this will do for now," remembering what they discussed earlier about Leo being the weak link. Thompson said, "Didn't you find that under Leo's seat?"

Catching his partner's hint, he said, "Sure did." They both looked at Leo and he dropped his head. He knows how dirty these two plays and he knew he was in trouble, unless Doe be 21, but he doubted that because he's a convicted felon and he had never been locked up, so he's going to probably want him to take the charge anyway, but "I ain't going out like that," he said.

The officers walked over and stood in front of them. "Well fellas, y'all got one of two choices, this here can go away, and I know you want that Doe cause you're a convicted felon," Thompson said.

"See, we don't want y'all, we want Cordell. You give us Cordell, we'll make this gun disappear, along with this," Weaver said looking around to see if anyone was watching, then pulling out an ounce of crack cocaine from his pocket.

Doe tried to jump up but couldn't manage with the cuffs on. "That shit ain't ours! Man, y'all fucked up, this shit is crazy."

"Like we were saying, we can make all this go away, all you got to do is give up Cordell," said Weaver.

"I ain't no motherfucking rat and y'all ain't going to get away with this bullshit," Doe shouted.

"Well partner, it looks like they have chosen choice number two, let's run them in," Thompson said.

"What about you Leo? You got something for us?" asked Weaver.

Leo sat over on the curb with his chin to his chest and they could almost see the tears forming in his eyes as he just stared at the ground and didn't say a word.

"I take that as a no?" Weaver said. "But if you so happen to change your mind, here's my number and I take collect calls," he stated as he put the cards in each of their pockets.

They waited until officers in uniforms pulled up. They gave them the paperwork then loaded Doe and Leo in the police car.

"What about my car?" Doe said.

"I guess it will be here when you get out," said Thompson.

"Are you going to at least lock it up?" said Doe.

"It ain't my shit," said Weaver.

"That's fucked up, y'all are some real pieces of shit," said Doe as he was pushed into the police cruiser.

They laughed, then got in their car and pulled off. "Which one you think going to call us first?" Thompson asked.

"Ten to one, it's Leo," Weaver said.

"I'll take Doe," said Thompson.

Cordell's phone rang and he moved away from the music to answer it. "Hello," he said into the receiver, covering up the other ear with his hand.

"Where you at baby?" Gina asked.

"We're at the car wash. Why, what's up?" he could tell by her voice that something was wrong.

"Doe just called collect. Him and Leo got locked up, he said something about a pistol and the Narcs planted some dope on them," she said.

"When did this happen?"

"I would say about two or three hours ago."

He thought for a minute and couldn't remember when the last time was he talked to Doe. He remembered Doe being out of dope, so he was sure the cops planted it on him like he said. Unless he went somewhere else and tried to get on and got knocked in the process.

"Did he say what his bond was?" Cordell asked, knowing it would be sky high with a gun and some dope.

"Nope, he just said what I told you."

"Call up there, find out and then hit me back," he said.

He walked back over to Chew and Moody and told them what happened.

"That's fucked up, I bet it was Thompson and Weaver. They the only ones that would do some shit like that," Chew said.

"You mean they are planting dope on niggas down here too? I got away from Hop-town cause of how they did me and I moved into some more of that shit?" Moody said.

"Them dick suckers Thompson and Weaver been trying to get at me for years. They know I ain't going for that shit, putting something on me," said Cordell.

"So what's up with your boys, are they solid?" asked Moody very concerned.

"Them niggas know I'll bury them if they rat on me or anybody I fuck with," Cordell said.

"You should've left them niggas alone a long time ago. I don't trust them niggas, plus, you know Leo's still fucked up about that ass whipping," Chew said.

"I'm waiting on Gina to call back so I can find out what they charged with and what their bonds are."

"Yeah, we might have to bond them niggas out then murder them," said Moody.

"Especially that bitch ass nigga Leo," Chew added with pure hate for him.

Cordell knew in his heart this was possibly true and that Leo would be the one to tell when it was all said and done.

Now that he looked back on that situation with Leo, he regretted not killing him then. He felt it was going to come back on him. He just hoped he could get to him before it does.

Cordell's phone rang. "Hello," he said. "Damn!" then hung up. "That was Gina, she said them niggas were charged with possession of a handgun while trafficking in crack cocaine and their bond is a hundred thousand a piece."

"How we going to post two hundred thousand without drawing attention?" asked Moody.

"I know!" Cordell said, "I'm going to try and see if Romone Scott can get the bond lowered in the morning, so we can get them niggas out and take care of them."

"Know that's right!" said Chew.

Cordell was up early that morning cause he couldn't sleep. He was tossing and turning all night and Gina even tried to assure him it was going to be alright.

For some reason he didn't believe that. How was these niggas so stupid to be driving around with a gun on them. "I can't say nothing, I do it all the time," he thought.

If Romone can get their bonds at 10%, that would be good, and we can get them out. The Feds won't sweat $20,000 like they would $200,000. "I wish we still had bail bondsmen, them niggas would have been out," he said.

He pulled up in front of the courthouse and got out. He saw all the police, which made him nervous, even though he hadn't done anything wrong.

He went through the metal detectors and headed for the courtroom where arraignments are held.

Romone tried everything he could, but couldn't get their bonds lowered or 10% and he could see the frustration in their eyes.

One of the deputies grabbed Doe and the other grabbed Leo and led them out of the court, back to the holding cells. They looked back at him and he met their glance. He could see the anger in their eyes, especially Leo's and he knew he had to get them out of there before they found their own way, and it would most likely be him. He couldn't post $200,000 even though he had it.

He waited outside the courtroom for Romone. Officer Thompson and Officer Weaver came out. They both looked at Cordell with the same shit eating grin that officer who had done his inventory in prison had on his face. This brought a cold chill to Cordell and he had a bad feeling and knew exactly what it was. "I'll be damned if I spend the rest of my life in prison," he said. He knew he had to kill Leo and maybe even Doe or that is what he would end up doing, life.

Romone finally came out of the courtroom. Cordell walked up to him. "Hey Romone."

"How you doing, Mr. Jenkins?"

"So, what's the deal. How can I get my niggas out of there?"

"Well, I tell you Mr. Jenkins, this is going to be a hard case to fight and for some reason, the Judge doesn't want to lower their bonds."

"Didn't Doe tell you how they put that dope in the car? They can't get away with that, can they?"

"The problem with that is no one saw them do it and though we know they're crooked as hell, the jury would not know what and if it went that far. They both would end up with a lot of time."

The thought of that had Cordell's mind racing because he knew Leo would give him up to save his own ass. "What about if I give you the money with a little extra, can you post their bonds?" Cordell asked.

"I'm afraid I can't do that. How would I look as their attorney if I post $200,000 for them. They'll bring me up on charges as well."

"So, what the fuck am I supposed to do?"

"Find someone who can post that kind of money without drawing attention to themselves or wait about two weeks and I can shoot the case to circuit court and we might be able to get a bond reduction there," said Romone.

Cordell thought for a minute. "Two weeks. I don't think I got two weeks," he said to himself. "Do you have anybody who can post this kind of bond without the attention?"

"Mr. Jenkins, to be honest with you, I don't think nobody I know would touch this because Thompson and Weaver are on it. Do you know the trouble that could bring?"

CHAPTER 20

Cordell looked at his watch. It was 3:30 p.m. He figured Doe and Leo would be out of court by now. He had been sweating the last two weeks and blowing Romone's phone up.

He dialed Romone's cellphone.

"Hello."

"Romone, this is Cordell. What's the word?"

"The Judge wouldn't reduce their bonds today and set a hearing for next week to see what kind of evidence they got. We might have a chance then, but I doubt it."

"So, it's looking that bad, huh?"

"I'm afraid so. It would be different if the witnesses weren't police officers."

He didn't have to say no more. Cordell knew what he meant. He was talking about his situation and how the witnesses change their stories. He got 10 years for two murders, but he knew that wouldn't be the case for Doe and Leo.

"Yeah, I know what you mean," said Cordell. "Just see what you can do for them."

"I always do my best, Mr. Jenkins," he said before he hung up.

No sooner than Cordell pushed the off button on his cellphone, the house phone rang.

"Hello."

It was a collect call from Doe. He pushed two and they were connected. "I've been waiting on you to call," Cordell said. "I just hung up with Romone and he told me y'all have a hearing next week to see what kind of evidence they got."

"What kind of evidence they got?" Doe said, with a worried tone. "Shit! I tell you what they got, an ounce of crack cocaine them rotten dick suckers planted on us and a hot ass gun."

"I understand that," Cordell said trying to be calm. "I'm trying everything possible to get y'all out of there."

"I'm cool. It's Leo I'm worried about, he's losing his mind. You know it's his first time being locked up."

"Is he there with you?"

"Yeah, he's right here."

"Put him on the phone," said Cordell, not knowing what to say. He started to tell him the truth, if you tell on me I'm going to kill you, but he knew the phones would record. "Leo, what's up?"

"Shit, waiting to get out of this hell hole. Why are we still in here?" said Leo, knowing the only reason Cordell wanted to talk to him was to keep him from telling on him. For the first time Leo thought about the card in his pocket.

"Look man, it's not that simple. People ain't got that type of money laying around. The ones who do are afraid it would draw too much heat," said Cordell, hoping Leo caught on to his hint?

"All I know is I've been in here for three weeks for some bullshit and I want to get out."

"Trust me, I'm doing everything possible to get y'all out," Cordell said. "So, I can kill you," he thought.

"The phone is getting ready to hang up, just see what you can do to get us out of here."

"I got you," Cordell said before the line went dead.

Leo turned and faced Doe when he hung up the phone. "What the fuck he means, people ain't got that kind of money laying around. Him and them niggas are fucking millionaires, two hundred thousand ain't shit."

"It's not that easy Leo. If a motherfucker came up here with two hundred thousand in cash and can't account for it legally, the Feds and everybody else will be on their asses."

"So, what are we supposed to do?"

"Shit, if we don't get our bonds lowered at the hearing next week, I guess we are going to have to lay and see how this plays out."

"Ain't that a bitch!" Leo shouted.

As soon as the phone clicked off Cordell called Chew.

"What's up Cordell?" he said.

"I just got off the phone with Doe and Leo. Man, I don't know how much longer Leo is going to be able to hold out."

"Man, I told you to leave them lames alone a long time ago. Hold up! You are taking collect calls from them niggas?"

"I know that shit is recorded. I ain't no fish."

"You know niggas be using that phone to set motherfuckers up?"

"Yeah, I know. That is why I really didn't say too much, feel me."

"How Doe sounded?"

"He seems like he's alright."

"You know we got to kill him too? If we kill Leo, he might get mad and tell," Chew said.

"I know. I pretty much had that in mind, but we going to have to get both and at the same time," Cordell said.

"You know what floor they on at the jail? We need to put somebody on them to watch their every move."

"I think they on the fifth."

"My cousin's on the fifth," said Chew. "I'll get him to get in the dorm with those fools. That way, he can watch them."

"Think we can get to them in jail?"

"Naw, that would be too risky. Plus, it would draw a lot of heat to you."

"Well, we got to come up with something baby boy."

"Don't worry. We will," Chew said.

CHAPTER 21

A week later, Cordell was pulling out of Indi's parking lot when his phone vibrated against his hip.

"Hello."

"Where the fuck you at?" asked Chew.

"Getting something to eat. Why, what's up?"

"Man, them niggas got out today."

"How you know?"

"My cousin called. He said, out of the blue, they called their names and told them to pack up, that they were getting released."

"They wasn't supposed to go to court until Monday."

"I know. That is what fucked me up when he called and told me. I asked him did they get any special visits. He told me no, but Leo stayed on the phone."

"Let me call Doe's phone. I'll hit you back when I find something out."

"Be careful and watch what you say. That niggas shit could be tapped."

"I really ain't worried about Doe. It's Leo who got me worried."

"Remember, no matter what, they both must go."

"I feel that and trust me, I totally agree," Cordell said. "I just hope it ain't to late."

"It ain't never too late. A dead motherfucker can't tell," said Chew.

Cordell called Doe's phone. It was answered on the fourth ring.

"Hello," Doe said.

"Damn, you wasn't going to let a nigga know you was out?" said Cordell.

"Shit, I just got over the shock of getting out."

"I thought y'all wasn't supposed to go to court until Monday?"

"That's what I thought. Then they called a niggas name and said we were getting out."

"So, what happened? Did they lower y'all bonds or something?"

"To tell you the truth, I don't know what happened."

"Where is Leo?"

"I don't know. When we got out, he went his way and I went mine."

"You call Romone?"

"Yeah, but I couldn't reach him. I guess he was in court," said Doe.

"Catch up with Leo and we'll hook up later and figure out how to get y'all out of this mess," said Cordell, knowing exactly how to get them out of it.

"Alright. I'll call you when I catch up with him," said Doe. Then hung up.

Cordell pulled over on the side of the road and thought about what had just happened. Leo and Doe was out of jail, didn't got to court and he hasn't talked to Romone.

There was only one way to explain this and it was Leo decided to give him up, why else would they just let them out. We got to find him and quick.

He started the truck and pulled off. He picked up his phone and called Chew back.

Chew was on the phone with Moody, who had gone back to his hometown to take care of some business. "Hold on, my other line is clicking," Chew said to Moody.

"Hello."

"I just got off the phone with Doe," Cordell said.

"Hold up, I got Moody on the other line. Let me see if I can click him on if I can remember how this motherfucker works."

There was a soft beep, then Moody spoke.

"Hello," he said.

"Hold on Moody," Chew said. "Cordell."

"Yeah."

"Okay, we're all on here," said Chew.

"So, what that nigga have to say?" Moody asked.

"He's talking about he don't know what happened. He said all he knows is they came and told them to pack up, they were getting out," said Cordell.

"What did his lawyer say?" asked Chew.

"That's the thing. He ain't even talk to his lawyer, he claims," Cordell said.

"That shit don't sound right," said Chew. "They don't just up and let a motherfucker go."

"I know that's right," Cordell said, looking at the light blink on his caller I.D., letting him know somebody is trying to reach him. "Speaking of the devil, that's Doe right there."

"Where?" asked Moody.

"On my other line. Let me hit y'all back," said Cordell as he pushed the send button to answer his other line. "Hello."

"I can't find Leo," said Doe.

"What the fuck you mean, you can't find Leo?"

"I called his house and his girl said he came in, packed some clothes and said he had to get a way for a little while."

"That bitch don't know where he went?"

"Naw, she said he didn't say nothing."

"Look Doe, I'm going to ask you a question, don't lie to me. Did he talk to them people?"

"Man, the whole time he was there, nobody came to see him or me."

"Do you know if he talked to anybody on the phone?"

"Not that I know of," Doe said nervously. "Why you ask that?"

"I was just wondering," said Cordell, not wanting to let Doe know he had someone watching them. "Look, see what you can find out and let me know?"

"Okay. Hey man, a nigga broke, that lawyer cost me and arm and a leg. I had to pay for Leo too. I need some work," Doe said.

"Right now, shit is slow. Let me see what I can do, and I'll hit you back. In the meantime, find out where Leo is," Cordell said.

"I'll do my best, but from the way his girl sounded, that nigga could be anywhere."

"Come on Doe, you and him been hanging together forever and I'm sure you know all his little spots," Cordell said trying not to get upset.

Thinking real hard cause he could tell from Cordell's voice that he's getting upset, he said, "There is one more place that I can try."

"You check that out and get back with me as soon as you find out something, so we can try to straighten this mess out."

"Got you man," Doe said, and the line was disconnected.

Immediately Cordell called Chew's phone back.

"Hello," said Chew

"You still got Moody on the phone?" asked Cordell.

"Yeah, let me click him in," said Chew. "Moody."

"Yeah, I'm here," Moody answered.

"Cordell," asked Chew.

"Yeah," Cordell said.

"Okay, we're on here. Shit, you never know with these phones. A nigga needs a college degree to work them," said Chew. "So, what's up?"

"Doe can't find Leo."

Before Cordell could finish, Moody asked, "what you mean can't find him?"

"That's what I said. His girl said he packed up and said he needed to get away for a while."

"I wonder why?" Chew said. "You got your shit clean?" he asked Cordell.

"I stay straight," he said. "Dig this though, that nigga Doe asked me for some work. Said he's broke, he had to pay for his lawyer and Leo's."

"They got the same lawyer, don't they?" asked Chew.

"Yeah," said Cordell.

"So that's possible. You know he probably charged them an arm and a leg for this case," Moody said.

Cordell started laughing.

"What's so funny?" asked Moody.

"That's exactly what Doe said. He charged him an arm and a leg." They all started laughing.

"So more than likely, Leo done told and that's how they got out," Chew said.

"What do we do with Doe?" asked Moody.

"I don't think he said nothing. If he did, he would have left with Leo," Cordell said.

"I still think we should get rid of him," said Chew. "I'll do it for G.P."

"If we do that, we'll never find Leo. He'll really hide cause he knows if I would kill Doe, I'll kill him without a thought," said Cordell.

"You got a point there. So, what about the work Doe wanted?" asked Moody.

"I'll just play him for a couple of days and see what's up," Cordell said.

"Just keep your shit straight," said Moody.

"We better all keep our shit straight. You never know what he told them people. You know how Thompson and Weaver play," said Chew. They all hung up and went to check their spots to make sure they were indeed straight.

CHAPTER 22

It had been a week. Doe had been calling Cordell everyday about some work and he didn't know how much longer he could keep putting him off before he became suspicious.

No one had heard from or seen Leo. Even with the $25,000 over his head there hadn't been a word of his where abouts. This was starting to worry Cordell. He had to find him and quick.

Cordell and Gina had just finished making love for what seemed like hours. He really needed that cause he was stressed.

"Where you going?" he said as he slapped her on her butt, as she was getting out of bed.

"None of your business. Why?" she answered, trying to turn her butt away from the playful slap.

"Okay, remember that when you call my phone and ask where I am at and I say that it's none of your business."

"You better not come home if you do," she said, as she disappeared out of the bedroom.

He relaxed and threw his hands behind his head. "This nigga Leo got my whole shit fucked up. A nigga can't make no money or nothing. Somebody got to find this motherfucker," he thought.

Gina was stopped butt naked in her tracks and Cordell was brought out of his thoughts by the sound of the door being kicked off the hinges.

The officers dressed in green jackets with the letters DEA, ATF and FBI wrote on them in yellow, stormed in with their guns drawn.

"Let me see your hands," one of the officers said to Gina as she stood frozen.

A couple of the officers, along with Thompson and Weaver had Cordell in the bedroom naked with his hands in the air. The rest of the officers searched the house.

"Cordell Jenkins, we have a warrant for your arrest and to search this residence," Thompson said, looking him dead in the eyes with the same shit eating grin he gave him in the courtroom.

Cordell didn't say a word or take his eyes off of Thompson. He was mad as hell, but he wasn't going to show it. They brought Gina into the bedroom and allowed them to put on some clothes.

Weaver walked up to him, "we got your ass now. I knew sooner or later you were going to fuck up."

"Our informant must be reliable judging by the way you're living," said Thompson. "They must be paying you good to be a flashlight cop. Maybe, I should get a job at the company you work for?"

"They say you the man in this city," Weaver said.

"Who said that? Leo!" he thought to himself. Then ignored their comments because he knew they were just trying to get him to bite. Maybe he would say something to incriminate himself. He remained calm and watched as the officers searched their room.

One of the officers in the green jackets came in the room holding a gun with his fingertips.

"Look what we got here," he said.

Cordell forgot about the gun he had under the bar in the basement. This still didn't worry him because, he knew the gun was clean. Plus, the gun was the least of his problems. He knew they didn't come here that deep to look for a gun. They haven't yet exposed their hand to him, but he knew in time they would.

Right on point, Officer Weaver asked, "Is that the gun you used to murder Capone?"

Weaver hoped that would have gotten a rise out of Cordell, but it didn't. Frustrated, he said, "Take his ass to the car."

"What are we going to do about her?" pointing to Gina, one of the officers asked Weaver.

"Let her go," he said, then got close to Cordell's ear, "I'll come back and fuck her later," loud enough that only Cordell could hear him.

Cordell was boiling inside and wanted so badly for a chance to beat the shit out of Officer Weaver, but he played it smooth. Like always, he'd find a way out of this.

They took him to Louisville Metro County Jail, where he was booked on the charges of first degree murder, trafficking in a controlled substance and possession of a handgun by a convicted felon. He remained there until the Feds came and picked him up a few days later and moved him to one of their hold overs.

He sat in jail for a few weeks, his attorney came to visit him often. His name was Alex Campbell. He first tried to get Romone to represent him, but Romone refused, sighting conflict of interest. He forgot he was representing that ratting ass nigga Leo.

Alex told him the case was next week, they were relying solely on the confidential informant who was yet to get a name. Cordell didn't need to hear that cause he already knew who the informant was. He couldn't get him a bond because of his previous record, so he would be in there at least until his trial.

Gina visited him every day and even brought Corchelle to see him. He hated it because she was older now and could really understand what was going on.

He didn't want his baby to see him caged up like some animal and couldn't touch him, but she wasn't having that and wanted to see her daddy. How could he deny his precious baby girl, and she might need to get used to it unless Moody and Chew could find Leo, which he doubted.

He believed the Feds had him put up somewhere in witness protection, that's why they couldn't find him. Now it was a waiting game, and may the best man win, he thought.

CHAPTER 23

"The Feds don't be playing," said Cordell, as he looked around the big ass courtroom. It had only been six months since he was arrested and here he was with his white button up shirt, black slacks, white and black tie and some Stacy Adams shoes on, ready to go to trial.

In State Court, a nigga could get shit laid over forever until he got to the witness or they got tired of fucking with them and cut a nigga a deal they couldn't refuse, he thought. Plus, if a motherfucker had a little money, he could buy his way out of State Court.

"I see why these motherfuckers got a 99 percent convict rate," Cordell said, still admiring his surroundings. He was overly impressed, considering the circumstances.

He looked up at the judge, who was white and looked to be around sixty years old. He had white hair, black glasses and was looking through some papers, probably Cordell's file because, occasionally he would look down at him.

He was sitting on a marble bench that covered from wall to wall. He sat so high up that Cordell had to hold his head back to look up at him.

The prosecutor was this funny looking guy named Charles Hester. He looked like he'd been beat up all his life by black people and now he was ready to get even. He would sometimes look over at Cordell and smile. "If we wasn't in this courtroom, I'd smack that shit eating grin right off of his face," Cordell thought to himself as he looked at the prosecutor and smiled back, showing no fear.

The desk Mr. Hester sat at with a slim lady with red hair was so far away from Cordell and his attorney, they had to use microphones to talk to each other.

The door in the back of the courtroom opened and Cordell saw his mother, Gina, Chew and Moody come in. He was surprised to see Moody and Chew, but thought they have nothing to be afraid of, cause they never really dealt with Leo.

Cordell was the only one who could bring them any harm and they knew that wasn't going to happen. He looked at Moody as Moody dropped his head letting Cordell know that they didn't find Leo.

At least when Leo comes in and gets on the stand, he would see them and know, one day he will pay for that.

He looked at his mother who looked like she hadn't slept. He could see the worry in her eyes, which almost made him cry. He knew he'd broken her heart yet again, but there was nothing he could do about it now. "I just hope someday I get another chance to do right by her," he thought as he turned his eyes away from her in shame.

He turned to Gina, who blew him a kiss and said, "I love you." He blew her a kiss and said the same.

Chew and Moody tapped their hearts with two fingers. That was a hood thing to say, "Much love my nigga." He did the same back.

The jury was called in and to his surprise, there were four blacks. He thought for sure it was going to be an all white jury. "Damn, I might have a chance," he said in a low voice to his attorney.

The jury was seated and the Judge ready the charges. Some of the white jurors looked at Cordell like he was the scum of the earth. The judge read them their instructions and the trial began.

The prosecutor went for the jugular right off the bat. He began his opening statement by calling Cordell a menace to society who didn't deserve to be on the streets or kept alive with the taxpayers money.

"Damn, that was harsh," Cordell said, eyeing the prosecutor with evil intent.

He went on about how not only was Cordell a murderer and drug dealer, but he had no respect for the law.

He brought up his two previous murder convictions, which his lawyer objected to because it was supposed to be restricted from the record, but it was too late because the jury had already heard it and it would be in their minds.

By the time Mr. Hester finished, he had painted a picture of Cordell Jenkins as this cold-blooded killer who sold drugs and didn't care about life or taking one.

Cordell could see in the eyes of the jurors, as they took in every word and even the black jurors were ready to hang him by his balls.

His attorney, Alex Campbell, opened his opening statement by degrading the kind of witnesses the prosecution intends to call. How their whole case is based on the lie of one man who would lie on his mother to get out of trouble.

Alex did a lot of damage control with his opening statement and Cordell could see the eyes of the jurors starting to soften again. He took a deep breath and started to feel like he had a chance again.

The prosecutor called witness after witness, police officers, lab technicians and even people who claimed to know Cordell that he never saw in his life.

"This cracker is trying to railroad me," Cordell said to himself, but loud enough that his attorney heard him.

"Mr. Jenkins, so far nobody has said anything that can hurt you. Who I'm worried about, is the informant," Mr. Campbell leaned over and said to him.

Finally, it was time for the prosecution's key witness, the confidential informant, Leo. He told the deputy to bring him in. So far, the prosecution's case was weak, just like Alex had said it was. Everything depended on what Leo had to say and Cordell knew it.

Everyone looked at the door in anticipation of seeing the one person who could send Cordell to prison for a very long time, if not for the rest of his life. His one-time best friend and now sworn enemy again.

The door opened and the deputy led the informant in, he walked in with confidence and arrogance. Cordell's mother's eyes widened with disbelief. Gina gasped for air at the sight of him. Moody and Chew looked on with pure hate and murder in their eyes as he walked past them, not even looking their way.

Cordell was the most shocked out of them all as he walked toward him looking him dead in his eyes and he had the nerve to smile at him. He wanted to come out of his seat. His attorney sensing it, tapped him on his leg.

The informant had on a black pin striped suit, white shirt, black tie and some black shoes. He took a seat and the judge asked him to raise his right hand, "Do you promise to tell the truth and nothing but the truth so help you God?"

"Yes, I do," he said.

"State your name for the record," the judge said.

Officer Weaver and Officer Thompson were seated in the back of the courtroom with those same shit-eating grins they had on their faces at the courthouse the day of Doe and Leo's arraignment.

The prosecutor looked over at Cordell, who was still in shock, with a smile on his face as the confidential informant said, "Norman Williams." The informant wasn't Leo, it was Doe.

CHAPTER 24
PRESENT

"Count time! Count time!" Smiley hollered as he locked the office door. It was 3:00, one of the four counts the institution has during the day.

Cordell looked at his watch and didn't realize how much time had passed since he came off visit. He stood at his door as the inmates are required to do during count.

Smiley walked past his door and off his walk, which indicated he was through with his count on that walk, so the inmates can continue doing whatever they were doing.

Cordell went back in his room and sat on his bed. "Damn, the whole time I thought it was Leo who was the confidential informant and it was Doe," he said to himself. "I know he's fucked up, I only got six years out of that shit and that nigga knows that I'm coming for him."

The jury came back with a verdict of not guilty on the murder and drug charges because Doe wasn't present when the murder happened, so all he could provide was hearsay and when he kept calling Cordell's phone, when he was wired, Cordell never said anything about drugs or provided him with any. Since they found the gun during a legal search, they found him guilty of possession of a handgun by a convicted felon. The jury recommended a five-year sentence, but the judge felt he was obligated to give him six years.

"Six years is better than the death penalty or life without," Cordell thought. "At least, I get a chance to get some get back. I just hope Chew and Moody carry out the plan just like I laid it out."

He thought about Leo and wondered what happened to him. He had heard that right after him and Doe got out, he was so scared, he bounced.

He thought they made a mistake and accidentally let them out. He didn't know Doe had called Officer Weaver collect and worked a deal for their freedom.

Now he's on the run, thinking they're looking for him and the case against him had been dropped and Doe got five years probation to testify against Cordell.

"I can respect running better than ratting," said Cordell. "So, I'm going to let Leo live, but Doe, that's a whole nother story, I promise you that."

The last four months went by so quickly that Cordell was surprised when he was called to the caseworker's office to get his merry-go-round papers.

He went to all the places he had to go to get signatures he needed to be released. He gathered all his belongings. This time it wasn't much because he didn't have his own TV, CD player, CD's and PlayStation.

Once in the property room he signed some papers and the officer escorted him out the door, down the walkway that he's came through when he first got there, and then out to the parking lot where Gina stood waiting him.

She saw him coming out of the gate, got out of her car and ran up to him. She gave him a hug and a kiss and then helped him put his stuff in the car.

He sat there without saying a word as he left the prison grounds. When he was at trial, he didn't think he would ever see the outside world again, but since the Feds do play by the book and don't try to railroad niggas, here he was once again, a free man.

"So, how does it feel Big Daddy?" Gina said, looking at him with a big smile on her face, happy to see her man.

"I tell you lil mama, I swear I never thought I was going to see this again when that nigga took the stand," said Cordell, taking a deep breath, enjoying the fresh air of freedom.

"That shocked the hell out of me when I saw Doe come through that door. I knew for sure Leo was the informant," she said, shaking her head still in disbelief.

"I know. The whole time this nigga was right in my face, acting like everything was cool. He even talked about how fucked up it was that Leo did some shit like that."

"Well, it's over now and you're out. Are you sure you want to do what you're talking about doing?" she asked him.

"Baby, I put my word out there and one thing I never do is break my word."

"But you know they're going to be watching you and if something happens to him you're going to be the first person they come to," said Gina.

"If Moody and Chew followed my plan like I told you to tell them, then everything should be good."

"I told them everything you said, and they said they got you."

"Then we have nothing to worry about and that nigga is going to pay for what he done."

They talked about Corchelle and everything that's been going on in his absence. About his mother, the new house and everything in between.

Cordell was sitting in the tub, trying to get the feel of five years of nothing but showers off of him. He laid his head back and let the hot water overtake him.

Gina walked in and sat on the edge of the tub, looking down at her man. The only man she had truly ever loved and had loved her in return.

"How does it feel baby?" she asked.

"I'm telling you I forgot what a bath feels like after five years of showers."

She smiled at him and playfully pushed water into his face and giggled.

"Oh, so you want to play?" said Cordell, grabbing her shirt, acting like he was going to pull her into the tub with him with her clothes on and all.

"Boy, you better not pull me into that water."

With a smirk on his face he pulled her into the tub as she tried her best to stop him, but to no avail were her efforts helpful.

"You're going to pay for that," she said getting out and removing her clothes to get back into the tub.

"I hope I do," he said, pulling her back to him with his arms tightly around her. "I love you lil mama!" he said as he kissed her on the neck.

"I love you too big daddy," as she laid her head back against his chest.

They sat there for a minute and enjoyed each other's touch. Then they dried off and walked to the bedroom, hand in hand.

He laid her softly down on the bed, pushed her hair from her face and tenderly kissed her lips as he caressed her breasts. Her nipples became extremely hard as he worked his way from her lips to her neck and slowly down the center of her chest. He grabbed her breast one by one and inserted her nipple into his mouth, running his tongue across them, sometimes slowly and other times fast. Occasionally, he would slightly bite them causing her body to jerk with pain and pleasure.

He left the breast and eased his tongue down to her stomach, in and out of her belly button. Anticipating where he would go next, she grabbed his head and started rubbing it.

From her stomach, he went to her inner thighs down to her kneecaps to her calves, down to her feet, where he took each toe, one by one and sucked on them.

He came back up and inserted two fingers in her warm wet pussy and slowly worked them in and out of her with a bend at the tip of his fingers for maximum pleasure. He ran his tongue across her clit, up and down then side to side, occasionally sucking it into his mouth.

He removed his fingers and dug his tongue deep inside her, tasting all of her juices. She moaned in pure pleasure as she clenched the sheets between her fists and came on his face.

He turned her over on her stomach and entered her from behind. Slowly he pushed his dick in and out of her, the strokes became faster and more passionate with each thrust of her hips.

She began to moan even louder, pushing her ass back and forth with his movements, taking in all his large black dick. She called out his name "Cordell, oooh baby, please don't stop," and he obliged her with deeper, faster strokes.

He gently grabbed a handful of her hair and pulled her head towards him and took the palm of his other hand and placed it in the middle of her back. Her ass moved higher in the air as he continued to pump with long intense strokes.

She gasped for air and took his dick like the strong black woman she is and they both came together.

He fell over on the bed, she rolled over next to him and grabbed his dick, it was still hard. "He wants to play some more, don't he?" she said as she put his dick in her warm mouth and began sucking it.

Unable to control himself, he came again, and she sucked every drop into her mouth and then swallowed his cum.

He pulled her up and kissed her passionately and held her like it wasn't going to be a tomorrow.

"There you go again," she said.

"What?" he asked.

"Kissing me like you're never going to see me again."

"Come here girl," he said as he kissed her again, but this time more slowly.

CHAPTER 25

The telephone rang and Cordell reached over to pick it up. "Hello," he said into the receiver.

"How does it feel to be a free man again?" the voice on the other end asked and he recognized it as his partner, Moody.

"Hey man, I'm telling you this shit feels so good, it makes a nigga want to cry, but I tell you what would make a nigga feel even better."

"What's that my nigga?" Moody asked before Cordell could finish the sentence, already knowing what he was going to say.

"For you to tell me you know exactly where that nigga Doe is," said Cordell, with anticipation that his requests were followed, and Moody knew.

"Now player, didn't you ask us to do something? Have we ever let you down?"

"Naw, can't say that y'all ever have," Cordell said with a huge smile on his face. "Come and get me."

"I'll be there in about 30 minutes and I got a surprise for you."

Cordell got out of bed, kissed Gina, then went and took a shower. As he put some clothes on he couldn't contain the rage he felt, knowing he was going to see Doe tonight for the first time since he testified against him.

He had Chew and Moody following Doe around for the last couple of weeks to see all of his hangouts and where he rested his head. He didn't want to have to search for him when he was ready to kill him. He knew he couldn't do it tonight because he thought about how it would look with him just getting out today, but he still wanted to see him, even if it was from a distance.

Gina rolled over and saw Cordell putting his shoes on. "You getting ready to go out?" she asked.

"Moody's on his way to pick me up, so I can get a look at Doe."

"You're not going to try and do nothing tonight are you Cordell?"

"Baby no, I'm just going to see him from a distance, that's all."

"Don't do nothing foolish, you just came home."

"I won't!" he said as he kissed her forehead and got up and went to the door.

He was in the doorway for two minutes, then Moody pulled up and before he could fully stop the car, Cordell was opening the door to get in.

"Damn, my nigga, you can't wait to see that nigga can you?" asked Moody with a devilish grin on his face.

Cordell looked at him as to say, what you think, then said, "He gets a free pass tonight, but before this week is out, that niggas dead."

"You know I got your back with whatever," Moody said. "Oh, by the way, here, you might need this," handing Cordell a nickel plated .40 caliber glock.

"This motherfucker here is cute," said Cordell, looking at the glock like it was a newborn baby. "Good looking."

"That's just one of the surprises," Moody said, knowing he had made his partner's day because he knew that Cordell loved guns and the .40 cal was a beauty. However, the other surprise was going to make the rest of his life sweet.

"Shit, I don't see how it can get any better than this," said Cordell, still admiring the glock.

"Trust me, it will."

For the first time Cordell realized they wasn't in Moody's caddy, but a rental. He was so happy to finally get to see Doe he wasn't paying any attention. That explained why Moody was riding around with the glock in the car cause he knew he wouldn't have it in his own car, the police could pull him over any minute if they saw his car.

They rode and he caught Cordell up on all that's being going on, the status of B.B.C. and the latest word on Leo, who still hasn't come back to Kentucky. Moody called Chew and told him they were on their way.

"Did y'all have trouble finding that ratting ass nigga?" asked Cordell, with anger in his voice.

"Naw, actually the nigga was riding around the city like he didn't have a care in the world, like he ain't done shit wrong."

"I'm surprised that nigga still here. I'm glad he didn't spot you following him."

"A couple of times we pulled right up beside him and the nigga acted like he saw a ghost, but we didn't say shit to him."

"That's good. I didn't want the nigga to get spooked and leave town cause then I would never find him," said Cordell.

Moody turned off Market Street onto a gravel road behind some houses off Northwestern Parkway. Cordell looked around wondering where they were going and what could possibly be back here that was a hangout of Doe's.

He thought maybe Doe lived in one of those houses, but when Moody turned on to a dirt road, he asked, "What's back here?"

"You'll see," answered Moody.

"This is the old Dude Ranch, ain't it?" Cordell said, as he saw the abandoned buildings and barns. "This motherfucker's been closed down since before I was born. My mother used to talk about how this place was back then."

Moody looked at him and shook his head, "Man just trust me. I told you I had a surprise for you."

Trusting Moody and Chew was one thing Cordell did and always would, but he still wondered what kind of surprise Moody had for him that would be back here?

They pulled up to one of the abandoned buildings, which looked like a double barn of some sort. There was a black F-150 sitting in the front of the building with a big ass wooden box on the bed.

Cordell didn't recognize the truck as anybody's he knew, but then again, he'd been gone for a minute. There was no telling what niggas were driving now.

What surprised him the most was the box. It looked like one of those old-fashioned coffins, but what would they be doing with a coffin back here?

CHAPTER 26

Moody turned the car off and told Cordell to come on. He checked the clip of the glock to make sure it was loaded, which it was and then Cordell stuck it in his waist. He slammed the door and followed Moody into the building.

The inside was very large and looked like it could fall in any minute. It was so old, and it was dark. The only light was coming from under a door toward the back and through the small cracks in the wall.

As they walked closer, he could smell what smelled like piss and shit mixed in with a strong body odor. Cordell stopped and pulled out the glock when he heard what sounded like a muffled scream and plea.

Then he heard a hard slap and Chew's voice. "What the fuck?" he said to himself.

Moody turned around and saw Cordell had the gun out. "You don't need that," he said to Cordell, then he pushed the door open.

Chew was standing in front of someone with their hands and feet bound with a rope and they were tied to a chair. He raised his hand and slapped him again as he smiled at Cordell. "What's up my nigga, welcome home," he said as he slapped the person again, looking like he was really enjoying himself.

From the inside Cordell could see that the man's face was swollen. His eyes were bleeding and completely shut. He was naked, all but the underwear he had on, which were yellow from the piss stains and brown with feces caked on them.

The smell was horrible, and many times Cordell and Moody had to grab their noses and shake their heads. Chew was either having so much fun that he didn't pay attention to the smell or he'd been here so long that he was used to it.

"Take a look," Chew said as he stepped away, slapping the man one more time for good measure.

Cordell moved around in front of the figure, through the swollen face, closed eyes and the only light being one of those big flashlights with the big battery, he could tell that the man sitting in the chair tied and gagged, was Doe.

"What the hell is this?" asked Cordell. "All I wanted y'all to do was follow him around and let me know his hangouts. That was the plan!"

"I know, but the opportunity was too sweet to pass up," Chew said with a little giggle.

"Shit, I'm the first motherfucker they going to pull in for questioning. How is this going to look? I get out of prison and this nigga come up missing in the same day?" Cordell said.

"I feel you, but you ain't got to worry about that," said Moody, moving around to get a closer look at Doe's face. "We snatched this nigga up two days ago, parked his car at the airport, bought two tickets to L.A. in his name, in which Chew's cousin and his girlfriend used. So, basically, he fled two days before you got out," said Moody, with a grin on his face like he done plotted the perfect murder.

Cordell shook his head in approval of the new plan and was so sure it would work, he wasn't able to control his smile.

He walked over and looked down at Doe in pure disgust. "What happened to him, not that I don't like his new look, but the nigga already looks dead."

Moody walked back over and took another look, shaking his head laughing. "You know how that nigga Chew is. Plus, he didn't like the nigga anyway," said Moody, still shaking his head feeling kind of sorry for Doe, but quickly dismissed the thought cause he's a rat.

"Y'all lucky the bitch nigga ain't dead!" said Chew. "When you left the nigga with me, you knew I was going to fuck him up."

Cordell took the gun from his waist and tapped Doe on the head. He didn't move, so he lifted his chin with the barrel of the glock. "Damn, how long you been beating him like this?" he asked.

"Oh, off and on for about 3 hours," said Chew, shrugging his shoulders.

"Nigga yo need some anger management," Moody said, looking at Chew.

Doe was finally able to open his eyes. He saw Cordell standing there looking down on him thankful it wasn't Chew. He knew he was going to die, but at least he wasn't going to get beat anymore before he did.

He tried to speak, so Cordell took the gag out of his mouth.

"I'm sorry!" Doe said softly with tears in his eyes.

"Nigga you're sorry!" shouted Cordell. "Nigga, you tried to get me a life sentence and all you can say is you're sorry." He took the butt of the glock and popped Doe in the side of the head with it.

Doe screamed in pain with what little sound he could muster, trying to keep conscious. "I didn't have a choice, they was going to try and give me 35 years for that stuff they planted on us."

"Do you remember what I told you if you ever told on me, that I would see you and murder you?" asked Cordell. "You told me that you would eat any charges that came your way and die in prison before you sign statements on a nigga."

"Please Cordell, Please!" cried Doe.

"I can't believe you. You've seen me put in too much work to know that I would kill you if you ever crossed me and now you want to sit here and beg," said Cordell. "You know my word is bond. Did you think I was going to let you get away?"

"What about my son, Cordell?" Doe said, trying to find some sympathy for his long-time friend.

"Your son! Nigga what about my daughter? Did you think about her before you tried to take my life?"

Chew was sitting there loving every minute of Doe's begging. He looked at Moody who also had a smile on his face. They knew it was only a matter of time before Cordell loses patience and puts that nigga out of his misery, but they had another plan in mind.

Cordell looked up and saw Moody and Chew coming back in with the wooden box. He had been so busy so busy fucking with Doe he didn't see them leave.

He looked on with suspicion and now realized what the box was for, but he still didn't know what was in the smaller box.

"Put the gag back in that niggas mouth and untie his bitch ass from the chair," said Chew.

Cordell put the gag back in Doe's mouth and untied him from the chair. Still with his feet and hands bound he tried to stand him up and move him over to the box.

Doe, knowing this was the end of his life, first tried to beg and plead with them as Cordell moved him closer to the box.

"Please Cordell," he tried to say through the gag.

"Nigga be a man, stop being a bitch you whole life," said Chew.

Seeing he wasn't getting nowhere with the approach, he tried to put up a fight as best he could, but with his hands and feet bound, it was useless. Cordell, tired of the games, popped him in the back of the head with the glock. He fell to the ground unconscious.

Cordell and Chew picked his fat ass up and threw him in the box. Moody grabbed the smaller box and emptied the contents into the box with Doe. Cordell jumped back as he saw all the rats trying to get out, it must have been 50 of them. Moody slammed the lid down and grabbed the nail gun and nailed it shut.

"Y'all are fucked up," said Cordell.

"Motherfucker want to be a rat, bury his ass with them," Moody said.

"Come on, let's get this out back and get this shit over with, so we can roll," said Chew.

All three of them lifted the box and felt Doe moving around frantically inside. "I guess he woke up," Chew said. Then they put the box in the grave they had dug and covered it back up.

"Come on, let's bounce," said Moody.

Cordell got in the car with Moody and Chew got in the truck.

"Once again, welcome home my nigga," Chew said as he pulled off bopping his head to the music.

When Cordell got home, Gina was waiting for him. When he opened the door, she ran to him and put her arms around him. "Did you see him?" she asked, worried that he might have done something foolish, like killed him in front of thousands of witnesses.

"Yeah, I saw him."

"You didn't do anything to him, did you?"

"Put it this way, you ain't got to worry about him telling on nobody else."

"You didn't do it in front of no witnesses, did you?" she asked, looking at him suspiciously because she knows he could be hot headed.

"Actually, Chew and Moody had a plan better than mine," he said, and he told her how it went down.

Turning her lips up at the thought of the rats, "Are you okay?" she asked.

"Yeah, I'm straight," he said, not really knowing if that's true. For the first time he had to kill somebody he was close to, but what choice did he have?

"Do you want something to drink?"

"Naw, but I would like to take a shower."

"I'll join you," she said as she started undressing him and then undressing herself.

They got in the shower and as he stood facing the water, letting it run over his head, she put her arms around him with her breast against his back.

"Well, I guess it's time to start making wedding plans," he said with a smile.

"Quit playing, Cordell, are you serious?"

"Baby girl, I told you when this was over, we were getting married. I gave you my word. When have you ever known me to break my word?" he said seriously. He turned to face, and she threw her arms around him and he did the same. He held her and thought about what he just said. For the first time in his life, he broke his word.

He promised himself that he would never trust another woman other than his mother and his daughter, but he trusted Gina. He trusted her with his secrets, his mind, his body, his soul and most importantly, he trusted her with his heart.

EXCERPT FROM "SHATTERED DREAMS II"

CHAPTER 1

Peter Gunnz, AKA the Gunman, and Fast Black sat on the corner in his black Impala watching Cordell's house.

Cordell pulled in his driveway in his silver Excursion, followed by some of his crew in a black Land Cruiser. As they exited the SUV's they looked around with their hands on the butts of their guns. This was more so a force of habit whenever they stopped somewhere. You never know who's laying in the cut waiting on you.

They knew nobody in the city was crazy enough to try them, at least they thought. Nobody noticed the black Impala sitting at the corner.

Ten minutes later, Moody pulled in with Chew on the passenger side in his gold 740 BMW. They got out and looked around as well. Moody noticed the dark colored car sitting at the corner, but he didn't see any heads, so he dismissed his suspicions. They entered the house where the rest of the crew were waiting on them.

Black, still low in his seat, asked the Gunman, "How many niggas Cordell have with him?"

The Gunman, looking through a pair of binoculars held up his index finger, as if to tell his partner to hold on for a second. He took the binoculars away from his eyes and said, "I saw Cordell and four more go into the house first, then Moody and Chew pulled in a little later. None of them had anything in their hands."

"Shit! Cordell always keeps six or seven motherfuckers around him when he's out," Black said, disappointed.

The Gunman processed those words and knew just like he thought six years ago, before Cordell went to prison, it would be almost impossible to hit them in the streets. Plus, he didn't want the pocket change them niggas carried around, even though their pocket change is most niggas house and car. He knew they were sitting on millions and that was the only reason that he was taking this chance.

When he first started plotting on these niggas, before Cordell caught that Fed bit, he thought it would be easy, but quickly learned these niggas stay on point. Even with Cordell gone it was hard. Now that he's back home, it was damn near impossible, but he had to try.

He took one more look at the house and then started the car, as he rode pass, he knew his day would come. He just hoped that he'd make the best of it.

Cordell and the crew were sitting at the large table in his den. They were discussing the shipment that's coming in from Miami this weekend. It was a total of 150 kilos of pure uncut cocaine.

All the men at this table trusted each other with their lives. Any betrayal or disloyalty would mean your life and they all knew this and knew how Cordell, Moody and Chew carried it. So they talked freely and recklessly among themselves.

"Tony, I want you to pick up the work and move it to the stash house. Once we know everything is everything, we'll move it to the Rock houses for it to be cooked up," said Moody, looking around the table.

Tony was Cordell's cousin and like Cordell, he was a killer. He was loyal and honest, his word was also his bond. His only weakness was beautiful women. Cordell used to tell him all the time, that that was going to be his downfall.

A slim cat named Polo, who supplied the west side of the city with drugs spoke up, "so how long do you think it would be before we can start putting this shit on the streets?" he said. "A lot of them been on hold for three days already."

"That's the same problem I got as well," said Shorty-Lo, a short fat dude who often ran with Chew, who handles most of the business on the south side of the city.

Looking around and understanding the readiness of their crew to get paper, Moody said, "If everything goes as planned by Saturday night, you all should be ready to grind." He could tell by the smiles on their faces they were satisfied.

"So, from now until Saturday morning, take care of all your business, do all your club hopping and fucking cause, come Saturday, it's all about chasing that dollar," Cordell said, looking into the eyes of everyone around the table and letting them know he was serious.

They all shook their heads in understanding and got up from the table, giving each other hugs and dap as they started to leave.

"Tone!" Cordell yelled after his cousin. Tony turned around and came back to him. "You especially make sure you're well rested cause we need you to be on your P's and Q's."

"You ain't got to worry about that, I'm good," he said as he tapped his cousin's hand that was laying on his shoulder.

Tone got behind the wheel of the Land Cruiser where Polo, Shorty-Lo and Face waited for him. He started the truck, pulled out his cellphone and called his freak Fe-Fe.

When he hung up the phone, Face looked at him, asking, "I just know you ain't still fucking with that scandalous bitch Fe-Fe?"

Tone, looking at him with wicked eyes cause he knew at one time Face was fucking her and he thought Face was just jealous. "Man, it ain't nothing but a fuck thing," he said. "Plus, she wasn't so scandalous when you were fucking her."

Face shook his head with a smile on his face, "Why you think I stopped fucking with that bitch?"

Neither one of them said another word about Fe-Fe, but instead, talked about the grinding they got ahead of them this weekend.

Tone dropped them all off at their houses or wherever they were going to chill, and then he went to Fe-Fe's house to enjoy the rest of the night.

Narcotics Officers Thompson and Weaver had been following Moody most of the day. They were surprised when they pulled up to the park a block from Cordell's house as

Moody turned into the driveway. They saw the black Impala parked on the corner in front of them.

They couldn't help but laugh to themselves because they knew who the black Impala belonged to. While they were watching Moody and Chew, the guys in the Impala were watching Cordell.

"Everybody in the city must know that dope is coming in soon," said Thompson, looking at the Impala.

"What you think we should do?" asked Weaver. "You know they got guns on them. There's no way Peter Gunnz is going to be sitting outside Cordell Jenkin's house and not be strapped."

"If we pull up on them, it would draw too much attention and blow our cover. How would it look, us and the Gunman outside of Cordell's house," said Thompson. "I've got an idea though. We've been trying to put Cordell and his crew away for a long time and I still don't believe Doe just up and left. He would at least sold his car and not left it at the airport. You know there's going to be a war if what we think is going to take place does."

Smiling at his partner without letting him finish, Weaver said, "Let them kill each other and then arrest the last man standing."

"We know the Gunman ain't stalking Cordell for nothing," said Thompson. "We can't get enough evidence for a jury to convict them, but in the end, if we catch the last man standing with a smoking gun, we got all the evidence we need."

"Better yet, you know none of them is going to drop a gun if they know they're caught red handed. So, they are going to hold court in the streets, and we can kill two birds with one stone," Weaver said while watching the Impala pull off without noticing them.

Moody and Chew pulled out of Cordell's driveway and made a left onto the street. They didn't notice the blue Crown Vic that was following them.

"What's up, you want to stop somewhere and have a drink?" Moody asked.

"Shit why not, this shit is going to be crazy this weekend. That drought hurt a lot of niggas, I'm just glad it didn't last that long," said Chew.

Black was about to take a shot at the eight ball to win the hundred dollars that him and the Gunman bet on the game when his cellphone rang. "Hello!" he said a little agitated. "Are you sure?" Then hung up the phone now with a smile on his face.

"Nigga what you are smiling about, shoot your shot," the Gunman said pointing at the pool table.

"Fuck that shot, start getting the crew together, we going to strike them niggas this weekend," said Black, then won the hundred dollars with two rails in the side bank shot.

"Do you think we need to call up them Brick City niggas?" asked the Gunman.

Corn and T-Dirty were two stick up kids who were young, but had plenty of heart and they were killers. They were from Cotta homes Projects and that's why they called themselves Brick City.

Whenever LMW or Brick City had a big job where they needed extra fire power and it was enough for everybody to eat, they would call on each other.

"It's enough for us all, why not," said Black. "Plus, we can use the extra fire power."

"That's exactly what I was thinking cause these B.B.C. niggas ain't just going to lay down and let a nigga take their shit," the Gunman said.

Moody pulled away from Club Ceder and was on his way to drop Chew off when he saw Mark standing at his car talking to some female. He blew his horn and waved.

He stopped at the red light and his phone rang. He looked at the caller I.D. and recognized Mark's number. "Damn, what this nigga want? I ain't going back," he said as he pushed send. "Hello." He hung up and looked in the rear-view mirror where he saw Thompson's Crown Vic. "Damn!"

Chew saw the look on his face and looked out of the side view mirror and saw what Moody was looking at. "How long they been following us?"

"I don't know. Mark just called me and said when we pulled off, they pulled off right behind us. Come to think about it, I thought that I saw that car earlier tonight when we were at Cordell's.

Chew had a concerned look on his face after hearing Moody's words. "You better call Cordell and let him know what's up," he said, still looking at the Narcs following them.

Early Saturday morning, Tone pulled up to the stash house. He opened the back of his Land Cruiser and took out three large bags. He had one on his shoulder and carried the other two in his hands.

This was the first time they used this house as a stash spot anyway. On a couple of occasions, Tone brought Fe-Fe over here to get his freak on. However, for this shipment, Cordell decided to use a different spot.

As he put his key in the door, after setting one of the bags sown, he heard footsteps running. Before he could turn around, he felt the clod steel at the back of his head.

"Nigga, you know what time it is, you seen this shit on T.V. You know what to do," someone said from behind the barrel of the gun.

Tone dropped the other bags and prayed these niggas didn't kill him over the bullshit in the bags. Sweat was running down his face as he closed his eyes and kept his head straight. He definitely wasn't expecting this.

Black grabbed the bags and handed one to Corn and they ran back to the car and threw them in the trunk. "Them motherfuckers were a little light," Black said to Corn.

"I know," said Corn, looking at Black with a curious look on his face.

The Gunman thought for a minute as he tried to decide if he should kill Tone or not. He knew he didn't get a good look at them cause they was on him before he could turn around. He knew if he killed him, being that he was Cordell's cousin,

Cordell wouldn't rest until he found out who did it. so he decided to slap him upside the head with the butt of the gun and leave him unconscious.

When Tone came to, he rubbed the back of his head where he felt a big ass knot. He reached for his cellphone and noticed it wasn't there, neither was his jewelry or the money he had on him.

The keys were still in the door. So he locked the door, got in his truck and drove to Cordell's house.

LMW and Brick City was sitting around the table looking into the open bags. You could tell by the looks on their faces they couldn't believe what they were seeing.

"Look at this shit!" said the Gunman, looking at Black.

Tone walked into the house and went to the den where Cordell, Moody and Chew were sitting, waiting on a word from him. They were surprised to see him walk through the door.

"What's up?" asked Cordell, looking at him suspiciously.

Taking a seat in an empty chair at the table, shaking his head, Tone said, Man you ain't going to believe this shit? As soon as I stuck my key into the door, I felt a gun at the back of my head. The nigga told me to drop the bags, then two other niggas picked them up and took off. Then the nigga with the gun took my phone, jewelry and money and hit me with the pistol."

Cordell, Moody and Chew looked at each other and fell out laughing. They laughed so hard they were on the floor. Tone couldn't help but laugh as well even though he could have lost his life.

"Hold up," said Cordell, trying to catch his breath. "Did you see who these niggas were?"

"Naw, I didn't see their faces, but I saw two cars when I pulled up. One was a dark Impala."

"A dark Impala!" said Chew, as he sat up in his chair. "I'll bet it was them LMW niggas, Peter Gunnz and that nigga Black."

"Yo, how did them niggas know about our stash spot to already be there when he pulled in and how did they know we were supposed to be there on today?" asked Moody very curiously.

"Nigga, who you been with the last couple of days?" Cordell asked his cousin, with a serious look on his face.

"Shit, I ain't been with nobody except my bitch Fe-Fe," Tone said, trying to assure them that it wasn't him who leaked the information.

They all looked at each other and knew Tone was a pillow talker and they all knew Fe-Fe and knew she was a slut that would do anything for a dollar.

"If I find out that bitch put some niggas up on us, I'm going to kill her and then I'm going to kill you! Family or not!" said Cordell.

"Damn man, they didn't get shit," Tone said knowing his cousin meant his words.

It was true, they didn't get shit cause when Moody told Cordell about Thompson and Weaver following them, they didn't want to take a chance.

So they had the connect drop the shipment off somewhere else and Cordell's wife Gina picked it up and took the work to a different spot. Then they put a bunch of books they were donating to the YMCA in the bags and had Tone to make the drop at the spot to see if Thompson and Weaver were on to them.

They didn't expect the stick-up boys to be the ones to be there and this made Cordell furious.

"The point ain't we didn't lose nothing. The point is a nigga was up on us cause some motherfucker opened his mouth." He said angrily. "Just think if Moody wouldn't have seen them dick suckers behind him and we had the work in those bags as planned, then what?"

Now looking stupid, Tone, looking down at the table, said, "I didn't realize that."

"You better find out if that bitch put them niggas up on us and if she did, you better kill her." Cordell said with murder in his voice.

"I'm getting ready to try and find out if it was LMW, if it was, them niggas are dead as well," said Chew pulling out his phone.

Cordell thought and knew it couldn't have been anybody else because nobody in the city had enough heart to try them, but those niggas. If that was the case, they just declared war. Nobody tries to take from the B.B.C. and lives to talk about it.

Cordell Jenkins was a promising young football star whose heart, ego and temper made him one of the most dominant forces to ever step on a football field in Louisville, Kentucky. He became one of the most sought-after players to ever come out of Kentucky. These same characteristics would also lead him to make decisions that would change his life forever.

His dream of playing in the NFL, could be shattered by the choices he makes and the people he encounters through this growing admiration of the street life. As life changing experiences come and tragedy strike, Cordell must weather the storms and go against a force stronger than he has ever faced on a football field.

As Cordell tries to put the pieces of his life back together, he finds that it's a lot harder than he could ever imagine. Though accomplishments have always been easy for him, the street might prove to be more then he can overcome.

Made in the USA
Monee, IL
05 April 2023

30785733R00095